PRAISE FOR SIMONETTI'S DEBUT NOVEL,
THE SOUND OF WINGS

"A story world so completely alive with characters so real,
I can feel them breathing behind me."

—Caroline Leavitt, *New York Times* ʰˡˡⁱⁿg author

"Reminiscent of Alice Hoffman in it
and sheer magic of its storytelling."

—Author Mary Morris, a   ɔr

"A charming and heartfelt debut
—Terry Lynn Thomas, *USA T*   ıthor

"....stirring....up to the touchⁱ

                                        Reviews

"A cast of characters that will stay with the reader long
after the last page is read."

—Author Patti Davis

"I lived for 30 years in Cape May and Simonetti captures
the seaside resort perfectly! If I could give this book 10
stars, I would!"

—*Amazon Reviewer 5-Stars*

"An undeniable page-turner that practically dares you
to set it down. From an author who just might be the
industry's best kept secret."

—*Indie Reader Reviews*

"The amount of emotion this debut has is enthralling."

—Reader Views Book Reviews 5-Stars

"The only rating this exceptionally well-edited book deserves is 4 out of 4 stars! The excellent writing, storyline, and editing make it impossible to provide any other rating."

—*Online Book Club Reviews*

"The author has expertly fleshed their backstories out in a way that by the end of the story, readers will feel that they've known the characters for a long time."

—*The BookLife Prize*

"If you are a fan of women's fiction, of books that will make you love the characters and wish the book didn't end, then The Sound of Wings is for you."

—*Funky Reader, Book Bub* review 5-Stars

A CAPE MAY CHRISTMAS STORY

A CAPE MAY
CHRISTMAS
STORY

A Celebration of Family and Love
in America's First Seaside Resort

[signature]

SUZANNE SIMONETTI

First Edition

Paperback: ISBN: 979-8-88896-717-1 $14.99
Ebook: ISBN: 979-8-88896-718-8

Library of Congress Control Number: 2023914578

This story is dedicated to all of my readers: Whether you are from one of the Carolinas, Pennsylvania, Las Vegas, Tennessee, New Jersey, or Canada, your love notes and book club photographs are a balm to my spirit. Thank you for taking a chance on my stories and sharing a piece of your lives with me.

AUTHOR'S NOTE

CAPE MAY IS CONSISTENTLY RECOGNIZED BY MAGA-
zine and trade publications. Just last year, *USA Today* named
the town as one of the top ten best small coastal towns by its
Readers' Choice Awards and in 2023 as No. 1 for best north-
eastern small towns for 2023. According to *Condé Nast
Traveler*, Cape May ranks among the top 27 most beautiful towns in America and stands at No. 9 in *Country Living
Magazine* as one of the prettiest spots in wintertime. *Globe
Trotter Travels* rated Cape May as one of the top 10 iconic
small towns in America and a great winter destination for
those seeking a relaxing getaway. More specifically, *Travel +
Leisure* believes Cape May to be one of the top 25 best towns
to visit in the USA at Christmastime.

Note: I have only mentioned a few here. The list is endless!

For centuries, travelers from all across the north-
east and beyond have arrived to the welcoming spirit of
America's first seaside resort. The crowds of the shop-lined
Washington Street Mall are not limited to the summer
months only. During the holiday season, the mall serves
up a festive display of cozy boutiques and fabulous dining

options, drawing visitors from near and far. Cape May innately captures the comfort and joy of the season with elaborate window displays and gaslit lamps. The town is imbued with a strong Victorian presence, which lends itself to the feel of a Charles Dickens classic. Every year, the Chamber of Commerce of Greater Cape May and Cape May MAC host Light Up Cape May, where judges award prizes for the categories of Best Residence, Best Business, Best Window, Best Olde Fashioned, Judge's Choice, and People's Choice.

Our story begins around a town treasure, which sets the stage for the holiday season: The West Cape May Community Christmas Parade held on the first Saturday in December. Now in its 58th year, the parade steps off at 5 p.m. sharp from the West Cape May Volunteer Firehouse, marches south on Broadway, turns east on Perry, and finishes at the end of Carpenters Lane in the city of Cape May. For a glimpse of how coveted this event is for the town, you will find many parade-goers setting up beach and stadium chairs all along the parade route on Friday afternoon, the day before the festivities take place.

During parade weekend, there are tree lighting ceremonies throughout the town. On Friday night, the crowd gathers at Rotary Park behind the mall for the annual city-sponsored Christmas tree lighting at 7 p.m. City officials host the event which includes live entertainment and a special appearance by the man of the hour: Santa Claus. If you miss the ceremony, not to worry. Simply head over to Congress Hall for their tree lighting at 8 p.m. and see how they transform the Grand Lawn into a seaside Winter Wonderland with tons of neat festivities for the kids and adults. Stop at The Original Fudge Kitchen for a sweet treat or to pick up a fudge-and-saltwater-taffy gift box. Enjoy a coffee or hot cocoa at Coffee Tyme at the mall or Magic Brain Café on Perry Street.

Many of the things I mentioned—*and so much more!*—will be captured throughout the book. I would run out of room if I tried to list it all here, and you have a story to read.

I wrote this book because seeing Christmas through the eyes of Cape May helps me to fall back in love with the season. There is a comforting charm here that is unique unto itself. Surely, I may have some readers booking their trips here for the holiday season. (Some friendly advice: The season books up quickly; make your plans well in advance.) In addition to the festivities, there are so many organizations around to help the unhoused, disenfranchised, and foster families. It's fun to play "Santa" to kids who wouldn't otherwise have a holiday. There is a list of organizations included at the end of this book if you wish to give back.

The Abernathy's Victorian home is purely fictional, as are the plot and characters. I hope the Abernathy family and my story fill you with the wonder I discovered when I first experienced that magic of Christmas in Cape May for myself. Whether it's the twinkle lights that take you back to childhood or a warm croissant from the local baker, may tidings of goodwill and peace surround you throughout the season and beyond.

Merry Christmas,
Suzanne Simonetti

PART I

THANKSGIVING WEEKEND

Rita

THE BEST LIFE SURPRISES ALWAYS ARRIVE WHEN LEAST expected.

And it wasn't a roomful of wrapped presents tucked beneath a Christmas tree, nor a row of full stockings dangling from a mantlepiece, that made the season bright. It was the memories—the ones made in the moment—that brought the real magic.

For many Christmases, Rita and Charles Abernathy took the ninety-minute drive from Brick Township with their two boys down to Cape May for a long weekend of festivities. Their family's official kick-off to the holiday season was always the West Cape May Christmas Parade on the first Saturday of December. Some of their most treasured memories were made up and down the cozy streets of the charming seaside town.

Many years had passed since those days. Now empty nesters, Rita and Charles were slowly being inched out of their old neighborhood in Ocean County as newer—and younger—families moved in. Most of the old crew who they'd raised their kids alongside had fled south to warmer states. Rita thought she might be ready for a change herself, yet didn't know quite what that might look like. Moving out of state was unthinkable to her; she was well-acclimated to four seasons. Just the same, with his retirement only a month away, a shift for her and Charles was imminent.

And then, without warning, Rita's life-changing surprise arrived on an impromptu day trip she and Charles took to Cape May. The previous December, they spent a Saturday afternoon enjoying the boutiques and restaurants of the Washington Street Mall. It was an unusually warm December day where sentiments of spring dangled awkwardly against the infinite gaiety of Christmas muzak. They ate, browsed, sniffed, and sampled their way through the shops, enchanted by the impeccably decorated window displays. On its worst day, Cape May was filled with charm and history. On its best, you knew you'd have to figure out a way to live there—and that's just what happened to Rita.

She found herself wide-eyed, standing before a Victorian home on Columbia Avenue with a *For Sale By Owner* sign mounted on a spike.

"Oh, please, Charles!" She tugged on his sleeve. "You know I've always wanted to live here."

"Hmm," he murmured, looking the house up and down.

Rita knew her husband's plan for retirement did not include saddling himself with a one-hundred-and-fifty-year-old Victorian home, but it had been her lifelong dream.

"Think of the Christmases we could have here!" she insisted.

For the past thirty-five years, Rita had enjoyed her career as a librarian. Being in Cape May at Christmastime was like walking through one of her favorite seasonal tales by Charles Dickens. The pages enveloped her into their story world like a warm hug. She simply couldn't get enough.

This magnificent, two-story Queen Anne Victorian in shades of russet, taupe, and sage green had an asymmetrical facade and steeply pitched rooflines.

Within minutes, the Abernathys were inside Clifford Bentley's foyer. He took great pride in lauding the home that had been in his late wife's family for three generations. The living room had nine-foot ceilings and stained-glass windows. Rita took one look at the enormous Christmas tree next to the ornamental fireplace and could almost hear her family gathered around in celebration.

The time had come for Mr. Bentley to sell and move closer to his only daughter who lived out west. As he walked them through the dining room, Charles noticed a large back wall of built-in cases with glass shelves.

"For the globes," he said quietly to Rita.

Her beloved snow globe collection was born the night Charles proposed, nearly forty years ago. He arrived at the library where she worked, wearing an overcoat in his family's tartan and a black top hat. The snow globe he gave her had a small Christmas village tucked inside and a secret compartment in the back where Charles hid the ring. Every Christmas since, he'd buy her a new snow globe with a special trinket inside such as earrings, an ornament for their tree, or show tickets.

Rita's globes were the first thing she unpacked when they moved into the house on Columbia Avenue last spring. Charles added lighting to showcase the magnificent collection which became a brilliant statement piece for their brand new dining room.

CHRISTMAS IN CAPE MAY WAS A TIMELESS CELEBRATION for the small town. Now being homeowners in the historic district, the Abernathys had the great fortune of joining in the grand experience for visitors and townspeople alike. Their home was featured as part of the candlelight walking tours first started by the Mid-Atlantic Center for the Arts in 1973.

During the tour, guests strolled the gaslit streets and enjoyed the holiday sounds of Christmas carolers as they made their way through more than a dozen homes, inns, B&Bs, churches, and hotels decked in holiday garb. It was Cape May's longest running and most popular Christmas tour. As a special holiday treat, Rita would serve hot chocolate in biodegradable cups to all visitors on the tour. Upon entering the breezeway, the entire five-bedroom home smelled like *Hersheypark* in Pennsylvania.

The previous year, *The Lorelei* on Perry Street won the Historic House Tour Award. The owner had received a congressional proclamation in tribute. The home was in a prime location where the horses rode by with their carriages on their way to town, before returning to their barn in West Cape May. Rita had high hopes of winning the honorable distinction this year. Being their first in Cape May, this Christmas held a considerable amount of importance to her for many reasons.

Their sons, Chase and Paul, were now in their mid-thirties and had gone in separate directions. Chase was her firstborn and her sunny adventurer. He ran an online travel blog featuring small-town life across America as seen from his RV.

Then there was Paul. He was a licensed plumber who had met his wife Shannon when they were twenty-two. Rita's first grandson, Miles, had just turned eleven, and her precious granddaughter, Tamra, was now six. With a house in suburbia, mounting bills, and a heavy workload, Paul had become the quintessential stressed-out family man.

Paul and Shannon were bringing the kids for parade weekend and Rita was ecstatic. She hoped being back in Cape May during the holiday season would remind Paul of the times he and his brother had so enjoyed when they were younger. The differences in their personalities had created a wedge between them. As the more serious son, Paul carried a lot on his shoulders, while Chase, who had always been the life of the party, seemed to have all the fun, friends, and freedom. Paul resented his older brother for this—a mother knows such things.

Rita closed the book she was reading as Charles entered the kitchen.

"Paul just phoned. We'll be joining them on Friday evening for pizza when they arrive," she said.

As part of their Christmas weekends in Cape May, Rita and Charles had always made *Lucky Bones* their first stop for the famous brick-oven, thin-crust pizza. It warmed her to see Paul carrying on the family tradition with his own children.

"How about some lunch?" Rita went to the stove and ladled soup into a tureen.

"Is that what I think it is?" Charles asked.

On snow days when the boys were younger, Rita would make a batch of Nonna's Italian wedding soup. Chase and Paul were winter hounds and spent hours building forts, pelting each other with snowballs, and riding their sleds. She'd have to lure them inside to thaw out. Nonna's soup always did the trick. It was the perfect snow day meal to warm up with, and it was a family favorite.

Rita could still see Chase and Paul in long johns and wool socks, slurping up the nourishing meal. The sentiment flooded her senses as she watched Charles warm his insides with the soup. Grandmothers had a way of leaving their imprints on special occasions, and Rita still ached for hers during the holidays.

Those were simpler times. There was a deep sense of contentment when the boys were growing up. They were the best of friends once. The wicked winds of time had changed all that. Chase was good about checking in but was usually off on some adventure, so the calls were brief. While

Paul was physically present, he was emotionally distant. Rita wanted nothing more than the whole family to be together for their first Christmas in Cape May, but Chase had already mentioned he wouldn't be able to make it home that year. She squelched the sadness rising in her chest and continued to observe Charles, lost in delightful oblivion.

"Soup okay?"

Charles pulled the napkin from his lap and dabbed the corners of his mouth.

"Your best yet. Grazie, Nonna!" He kissed his fingertips like a chef and looked up to the ceiling.

Rita smiled as she remembered the first time she brought Charles home to meet her family. Even Nonna—who was markedly leery of strangers and set in her ways—was endeared by the innate sense of wit Charles picked up from his father, who hailed from Edinburgh.

"Everything tastes better down here," she said as she ladled more soup into his bowl. "It's the magic of Cape May."

Charles paused momentarily to give her a sideways glance before returning to his soup. By season's end, if all went according to plan, Rita would prove to her stubborn husband that there was, in fact, magic in the seaside paradise they now called home.

EGG HARBOR TOWNSHIP, NJ

THANKSGIVING WEEKEND

Paul

THE FRAYED RUBBER SOLE OF PAUL'S WORK BOOT caught the last step of the ladder. He tripped and smashed his shin against the side rail. He'd never remember the profanity he blurted, but his wife's face said it all.

"Honey, please! The neighbors ..." Shannon's clear blue eyes moved like ping-pong balls as she took in the surrounding houses.

He grumbled and rubbed his now-throbbing leg. Shannon followed as he limped across the front lawn, reached the driveway, and entered their two-car garage.

Paul knew he was just like any other suburban dad filled with agitation and exhaustion from spending the better part of Thanksgiving weekend stringing twinkle lights.

"The kids are really excited to see Cape May next weekend. Tamra is laying out her dresses and matching barrettes. Miles is excited to help Grandpa stack firewood."

Paul's jaw tensed. He had forgotten the Cape May Christmas Parade was already next week. Even off the clock, his life was filled with obligations. He had no time to himself.

"It'll be nice to see your parents again," Shannon said.

Paul wanted to point out that his parents had just been there two days earlier, but instead of doing so, he simply said, "Yeah."

"Maybe it will help to clear the air," she said.

He wasn't expecting that remark and didn't need to be reminded of losing his cool in front of his parents on Thanksgiving morning.

When Paul didn't say anything, Shannon wisely changed the subject.

"The team is launching a new cream designed specifically to reduce fine lines around the mouth," Shannon said and puckered her lips. "There's a patent out for the new technology which is safer and less expensive than Botox or fillers."

Paul just listened. Sometimes, he felt like he stumbled upon one of those late-night infomercials. He desperately wanted Shannon to have her own thing, but unfortunately, this new business endeavor cost more than it brought in.

"Any news on Tony?" Shannon asked.

Tony was Paul's boss. He wondered how his wife could so easily jump from one gut-churning subject to the next in the same conversation.

"I haven't seen him." Paul's boss hadn't been at the office much in the last few weeks, which concerned him.

Shannon nodded gently and reminded him that dinner would be ready at six o'clock. She glided back up the stairs to the house. Her long red braid swayed like a horse's tail.

The garage was a constant reminder of all the things Paul didn't have time for. The shelves were lined with labeled containers: *nails, screws, sundries*. The work bench from his father called to him from beneath lined rows of hand tools mounted on the wall. They'd spent countless weekends preparing the work area to create a space for Paul's weekend projects. It gnawed at him to see the space and equipment not being put to use. Too bad the stupid garage wasn't the only thing in his life making him raw.

For the last sixteen years, Paul worked for *Down the Shore Plumbing*. After he earned his plumber's license, the owner, Tony Jackson, hired him on the spot. Tony, a born and raised Philadelphian, had grit and street smarts, and Paul was determined to learn as much as he could from his new mentor. Over the years, Paul worked his way up in ranks, becoming their top plumber and the first guy the dispatchers called if one of the plumbers needed help on a job.

The men had grown quite close over the years. Paul looked to Tony as a mentor who had a treasure trove of solid life advice he shared freely. He and Shannon had attended all three of Tony's daughters' weddings, the christenings for all six grandchildren, and spent time with Tony and his wife, Sheila, on their boat for sunset cruises and cocktails.

One weekend, Paul was running errands and headed to the office to drop off his paperwork. As he drove past the building, he saw Ralph Grayhall's unmistakable electric blue GMC truck parked out front. Ralph was the owner of *Tidal Wave Plumbing* and Tony's largest competitor. The two men kept up appearances and were cordial, but deep down they couldn't stand one other. It was a battle over territory. Tony had been well established in the marketplace until Grayhall expanded his own operation further south onto Tony's turf. Shannon referred to the men as frenemies since they were a combination of both.

As unusual as it was to see Tony anywhere near the office on the weekend, it was twice as strange to see Ralph Grayhall's truck at *Down the Shore Plumbing*. Paul waited until the following week, fully expecting some crazy story about how Ralph stopped by out of nowhere; but nothing was ever mentioned. It was as if the meeting had never happened—or Tony didn't want Paul to know anything about it.

What Paul did know was that Ralph Grayhall had been hungry to buy Tony out for years. As Tony rounded the corner on forty years in business, there was some talk about what his next move would be. Ralph had a fully trained and loyal staff. Paul would never survive a merger. While he didn't come right out and say it to Shannon, he was in serious danger of losing his job.

PAUL SCRUBBED HIS HANDS IN THE POWDER ROOM JUST off the kitchen. He heard Shannon ask Miles to remove his electronics from the table for the second time, which sparked a flicker of irritation. He tried to recall if he was this big of a pain at age eleven. Between his son's sporadic mood swings and brooding, raising Miles was like running the gauntlet. In a way, Paul was glad Tamra was five years younger. He didn't think he and Shannon could handle raising two tweens at the same time. Maybe they'd be better prepared when it was their little girl's turn to drive them bonkers.

A stack of construction paper and colored pencils covered Paul's placemat at the dinner table.

"Is this a party for three?" he said.

Shannon turned around in confusion and noticed the mess in front of her husband's seat.

"Tamra, please clear your artwork from the table so Daddy can join us."

Paul was too tired to deal. He just wanted food, a hot shower, and to maybe catch the last quarter of the Eagles game before another crappy week of work began.

He felt Shannon's eyes upon him.

"I was thinking I'd use the gift certificate your parents gave me last Mother's Day," she said. "The one for the day spa. It'll be nice to sneak away for a massage next weekend."

She added another helping of her famous one-pot shrimp dish to Miles' bowl after she noticed he had already plowed through his first serving.

"Slow down, dammit," Paul snapped at their son. "Take a breath."

Shannon sat back in her chair with a frown of disappointment. She had asked him to control his angry outbursts in front of the children.

"Anyway, I just wanted to remind you that I scheduled a massage for Saturday," she said.

This road trip was going to cost him. Shannon and the kids were indefinitely going to fall in love with Cape May—just like his parents had. When they were kids, he and his brother loved spending their summers and holidays there. Paul had brought Shannon there for a weekend getaway back when they were first dating, but she had yet to see the town at Christmastime. He almost dreaded the magnetic effect the enchanting beach town was going to have on his family.

"Will Uncle Chase be there?" Miles asked.

Shannon stopped chewing. Paul cleared his throat.

"Grammi said he wasn't going to be coming home this year," Paul said, hoping to end the subject.

"What about for Christmas?" Tamra said. "Uncle Chase has to be home when Santa Claus comes."

Miles snickered. Shannon shot him a warning look. He should know better than to ruin the magic of the season for his little sister.

"We'll have to see," Paul said.

He excused himself and brought his dish to the sink before there was any more talk of his brother.

"You sure you've had enough to eat, honey?" Shannon's voice could be so sweet and angelic at times. It made his heart hurt.

"I'm sure," he said before leaving the kitchen.

Paul favored his injured shin as he walked slowly down the narrow hallway and noticed the family photos hanging on the wall. Most of the frames were titled and skewed—just like his whole life and everything in it.

I've had enough.

PARADE WEEKEND

Rita

RITA SCANNED THE PILE OF BOOTS AND COATS HANG-ing from the rack in the breezeway. Having so many over-night guests brought a different feel to the space. Of course, she was happy to have the grandchildren there. Shannon was lovely. A reader like she and Charles, they were endeared to her from the start.

After Miles was born, Shannon and Paul had challenges becoming pregnant, which was why it took Tamra five years to arrive. Her daughter-in-law had handled the difficulties with grace and had eventually given Rita and Charles two beautiful grandchildren. There wasn't anything she and Charles wouldn't do for Shannon.

Rita's greatest concern was Paul's growing impatience with the kids and nearly everything he tackled. Last week for Thanksgiving, Shannon led the charge and orchestrated the whole menu. Paul was having a difficult time carving the turkey and snapped at Miles. Charles tried to assist which only sent Paul storming out of the kitchen. Rita felt terrible, especially for poor Shannon; she knew what it was like to be the epicenter of everyone's holiday as wife and mom and spend all that time and energy on an elaborate feast.

Earlier that afternoon, Paul had unloaded the car with the same amount of malcontent, and Rita cringed. She had stayed inside with Charles since they only seemed to get in the way. She didn't know why Paul was carrying so much angst, but his stress levels were alarming.

Rita still remembered the carefree, energetic boys who would jump off the bus, dump their book bags, wash down ham and cheddar cheese sandwiches with apple juice, and run right back out the door. Back then, their neighborhood was filled with kids playing and exploring. Rita remembered how she and Charles deliberated buying the Nintendo game system one Christmas. As bookworms, it challenged their sensibilities to permit such a mind-numbing noisemaker in the house when they had full access to the library. That year, both boys had earned high marks on their report cards, and since all their friends already had the game system, Santa Claus came through for the Abernathy boys. One thing Rita always got right: knowing how to make Christmas special. She longed for those days, wishing she still had her special Mommy powers to fix things for her sons.

"Mom! Did you bring the charger for my iPad?" Miles called out from the upstairs guest bedroom.

Rita wasn't accustomed to sipping her afternoon tea with commotion in the house. She thought it absurd to have to carry electronic equipment when there was so much wonder to be had in Cape May.

"Is it Mom's job to make sure you pack all your things?" Paul's voice boomed down the hallway.

He could intimidate. Even Rita shrunk an inch in her seat.

"I put it in the bag with all the other chargers," Shannon said, joining Rita in the parlor.

"I forgot what it was like having young boys in the house," Rita said, not unkindly.

"Miles can be a handful. I'm sorry if we're being too loud," Shannon said. "He's changed so much this last year. It's like someone came along and stole my sweet boy, replacing him with this *pre-teen*."

They both laughed.

"I know what it's like to be the mother of pre-teens. That does sound like a dirty word, doesn't it?" Rita said.

"That's because it is." Shannon helped herself to a tea cup and sat down at the table. "I don't know how to reach him. It's like we don't speak the same language anymore."

"Miles is in a transitional period. He's facing a brand new chapter to manhood while trying to shed his childhood persona that he doesn't even know exists. He won't realize any of this until his growth spurt is behind him. Like I said, he's facing a new chapter."

"I know all about facing new chapters," Shannon said wearily.

"What's happening with the face cream business?" Rita asked.

"It's a whole skincare line." Shannon visibly perked up. "The company founded this innovative technology. It's new to the industry. There's a patent now and everything. We're just waiting for approval. The trials have been amazing. People are getting great results."

"You sound passionate about the product. They're lucky to have you on board."

Rita meant it. Shannon approached most things with the same unbridled enthusiasm as she did motherhood—she was a sure bet.

"How does it work?" Rita asked. "Is it like one of those old pyramid schemes?"

"Not exactly. It's a direct sales and marketing company that specializes in skincare products," Shannon said. "They call it multi-level marketing. I make money on sales, not for signing people up."

"How many clients do you have?"

"Four. It would have been six, but two of the class moms flaked out just before our meeting. I have my sister and her book club to thank. I love women who read. They always seem to know what's going on."

"Hmm. Maybe I'm not reading enough." Rita teased, making a silly face.

"Oh, sure. Says the librarian," Shannon said.

"So, tell me more about this new chapter you're facing."

Shannon grew pensive. "You see how big the kids are getting. They don't need me as much anymore."

"That does happen, yes," Rita agreed.

"I accept that they're not babies. I mean, I still choke up when I look at their first-day-of-school photos, but I love having more time to myself, and I definitely don't miss the potty-training phase."

"Sounds like this new business venture came at just the right time."

"I guess so."

"Honey, can you shed some light on what's happening with Paul? I've tried asking—gently, of course—but you know how he can be," Rita said. "He closes right up."

"There's some stuff going on with Tony at work," Shannon said.

Rita thought for a moment. "Tony? I thought he loved Tony."

"He does. Paul saw Ralph Grayhall's truck parked at the office a few weeks back on a Saturday. There's a rumor that he wants to buy Tony out."

"Oh, gosh. No wonder Paul is so on-edge. I'm glad you told me this."

Rita wrung her hands. When she had a moment alone, she would think about how to help Paul.

"I'd like to be your fifth customer," Rita said.

"Oh!" Shannon waved a hand. "You don't have to do that."

"Why not? I'm a woman. An aging woman. I need good face cream just as much as the next old fogey."

"You are *not* an old fogey!" Shannon's face took on an elfin appearance when she giggled.

"And that other son of mine," Rita said. "Have you seen what he's been up to?"

Chase had a large online following. His travel blog was called *Chasing the Dream*. Shannon and the kids were among his loyal social media followers.

"Let me check to see where he last touched down."

Shannon pulled out her phone and began tapping and swiping.

"Last week, he was in Raleigh. Yesterday, he was at a winery near the Chesapeake Bay in Virginia."

Rita's heart did the two-step. Was it possible that her son was working his way up the eastern seaboard? She hated to get her hopes up. He told her last month that there was no way he'd be able to make it home in time for parade weekend. To believe otherwise was a risk.

"Can you give me any hints on what you and Charles may want for Christmas?" Shannon asked.

Rita thought for a moment. What she wanted couldn't be bought.

"I already have everything I need," she said quietly.

Shannon gave her a kind but dubious grin.

PARADE WEEKEND

Paul

AFTER A LONG WEEK OF WORK, PAUL WAS NOW TRAPPED in a snow globe of merriment and holiday cheer. It was fun visiting Cape May as a kid, but with all the uncertainty at work, he had a hard time enjoying much of anything these days. He started to identify with Clark Griswold, that absurdly funny character played by Chevy Chase in *National Lampoon's Christmas Vacation*. Only there was much more at stake than a yearly bonus—Paul's livelihood was dangling above an abyss.

"Daddy?" Tamra plopped down hard onto the large bed in the guest room. She was holding a picture frame. "Is this you and Uncle Chase?"

"You can't go jumping around on Grammi's new beds like this. I need you guys to behave this weekend. All right?"

Tamra pouted.

Paul took the photograph from her for a closer look. "Yes, that's us," he said.

"Where were you?"

It was the summer of '98. Chase had just turned eleven, and Paul was nine. Of course, his brother had somehow made friends with beach patrol and scored two T-shirts. It was one of the best beach days Paul could remember.

"Decatur Beach. This was taken right here in Cape May." Paul handed the framed photo back to his daughter. "That's a rescue boat we're standing next to."

"What's a rescue boat?" she said.

"It's what the lifeguards use to save swimmers who might be in trouble out on the water."

Tamra scrunched up her face in that same adorable way her mother did.

"Daddy?"

"Yes, baby?"

"Do you like Uncle Chase?"

"Of course I do, sweetheart. Why?"

"It doesn't seem like you would be friends or something."

Paul considered this for a beat before he changed the subject. "Speaking of brothers, where's yours?"

"Umm, I don't know." Tamra hopped off the bed and pranced out of the room.

Things seemed easier even just a year ago. Questions like *What's a payphone?* had less of an effect on Paul's stomach than *Why is Uncle Chase so fun and you aren't, Daddy?*

His brother ran some sort of a travel blog and had a large internet following which included Shannon and the kids. In excruciating detail, Paul got a rundown of all the places Chase went and every frivolous video he shared. At thirty-four years old, Paul was still living in his older brother's shadow. The whole scenario wore him down and pissed him off.

Just after they brought Tamra home from the hospital, Chase came to stay with them, in one of his infamous and unexpected drop-ins. He was in between destinations and had some time to spare. Miles had started kindergarten, Tamra was just born, and Shannon was on mandatory bed rest after complications with her delivery. Chase came to see the new baby, bearing souvenirs for every one of them.

There was a sense of joy hearing Miles squeal with delight every time his uncle entered the room. Shannon loved that Chase was there to entertain Miles while she healed and tended to her newborn baby girl.

After about a week, it was time for Uncle Chase to move on, leaving just as abruptly as he had arrived. Miles was crushed, as was Shannon. Paul had the feeling that his family was being used as a pit stop between adventures. He wondered if his brother knew of the wake he left every time he sailed off to his next destination.

Chase had always gone his own way. People gravitated toward his happy-go-lucky, carefree attitude, and he never had a problem finding friends. Paul wouldn't even know if there was anyone special in his brother's life. They'd been out of contact for several years. The more he thought about it, the more he realized just how little he and his brother knew of each other. An unfamiliar melancholy seeped through his chest like a noxious gas.

Tree branches brushed up against the wood shingles. Paul thought his parents were out of their minds when they moved to Cape May. All the other parents from the old neighborhood either stayed in their family homes or downsized in another state. They didn't retire, sell everything, and buy a one-hundred-and-fifty-year-old Victorian. But his mom had fallen pretty hard for the place. She was on some mission to win a prize from the town for being the best-decorated home. After Tamra was born, his mother went through a bit of a crafty phase. Every visit with the kids, Grammi would be ready and waiting with all her supplies and gadgets. One year, she had the entire kitchen and living area staged like a home-ec classroom, with paint brushes and easels, beads and glue. They'd spend the day making crafts, baking cookies, and then put on a performance with costumes. Being surrounded by stories for all those years in the library fed his mother's fanciful imagination. Paul shouldn't have been all that surprised his parents had pooled their resources and splurged on the Victorian.

The chimes echoed through the hallways. Someone was at the front door. Paul checked his phone on impulse to see if he had any new messages, and waited. The chimes rang again.

Why isn't anyone answering the door? Where the heck is everyone?

He went to the front of the house, expecting to see the UPS guy as he pulled open the solid oak front door.

A man in a full-blown Santa Claus costume stood on the front porch with a large bag of gifts slung over one shoulder. Paul figured he was a volunteer from Cape May MAC and part of the act for the candlelight walking tour.

Before he could say anything to the man, Paul sensed some commotion behind him.

Suddenly, a gaggle of Abernathys—his parents, wife, and both kids—erupted into a chorus of excitement and hollers.

"Real good to see you again, bro," Chase said.

The silver bell attached to the pom-pom of his Santa Claus hat jingled in Paul's ear as his brother crossed the threshold.

PART II

*"Blessed is the season which engages the whole
world in a conspiracy of love."*
~Hamilton Wright Mabie~

PARADE WEEKEND

Patti

PATTI KELLEY WALKED THROUGH THE DARK AND RAINY side streets of Cape May back to her apartment. The colder months were a baker's best friend in a coastal town, as the frigid ocean air drew customers inside for fresh coffee and warm doughy delights.

Thanksgiving weekend depleted her inventory and emptied the front case display. She'd spent the entire week replenishing supplies and restocking the freezer with fresh dough balls, and it was a good thing she did—the town was already packed for parade weekend.

Before she bought the bakery, it was being run like a generic cafe with pre-made cakes and muffins. Patti was a trained pastry chef, or a *patissier,* as the French would say, and wanted to brand herself as such. She hired a local artist who made a wooden sign with a fresh coat of lacquer that hung above her storefront: *Patti's Pantry, Est. 2021*.

Patti had attended the Academy of Culinary Arts program at Atlantic Cape Community College for baking and pastry. It was top-rated, with more students in the state of New Jersey than any other culinary school. She was given a thorough mix of classroom training, kitchen laboratory experience, and externship experience.

During her time in culinary school, croissants were her go-to treats. Every morning and afternoon between classes, she'd luxuriate in the buttery goodness. Patti was so ecstatic to be doing what she loved; she didn't obsess over the extra pounds she gained. Her love handles were badges of honor, and receiving that diploma was the key to her future—a future that included owning a bakery where trays of croissants slid in and out of the oven all day long. After years of hard work, she was finally living the dream.

PATTI SLIPPED OFF HER SNEAKERS AND DROPPED HER bone-weary body onto the loveseat. The raucous winds brushed the windowpanes, bringing an extra chill to the damp night.

So much for the Cape May bubble, she thought. Patti grew up in Bucks County, Pennsylvania, but her late mother was from Wildwood, next to Cape May. On occasion, she'd heard her mother mention this weather phenomenon, but

Patti had never known what it was until she moved to the town two years earlier. The *Cape May bubble* was used to describe situations where predicted storms or rain seemed to split, dissipate, or change course around the peninsula, leaving the area relatively unscathed while neighboring regions experienced the full force of the weather event.

Patti's phone pinged with a text from Rita Abernathy. Theirs was a special bond that went back to Rita's older sister and Patti's mother, who attended *Wildwood Catholic* together. She could hardly believe it when Rita moved to Cape May the year after she did. Even though Patti had only met Rita a few times in passing when she was a kid, it was comforting to have an old family friend nearby. There were times Patti wondered if her mother had sent Rita to look after her.

Rita: *How'd you make out this week, sweetie?*

Patti: *Restocked. Ready for the crowd.*

Rita: *I have some great news to share. My other son came home!*

Patti: *That's wonderful!*

Since the closing last January, Rita had been planning her first Christmas in the new house. Paul was visiting with his wife and their two kids, but the other son—whose name escaped her—was off traveling for work. Rita had been terribly upset that he wasn't going to make it home for the holidays, so this was welcome news. Patti was glad her friend was going to have the Christmas she'd been imagining since moving to Cape May.

The week before, Rita had dropped off a batch of Italian wedding soup and picked up a croissant assortment for Thanksgiving.

"You must be breaking some kind of city ordinance," Rita said. "The entire town smells like a bread factory."

"That's wonderful to hear," Patti said.

"Not so wonderful for those of us on diets." Rita eyed the case of baked goods. "I already pigged out on fudge."

"You're not supposed to diet during the holidays. That's why Santa Claus says to hold off on resolutions until January. It's all in the Christmas handbook," Patti said.

"The Christmas handbook?"

"That's right." Patti removed a tray of her famous almond scones.

"Oh, gosh, those smell terrific," Rita said. "How's business going?"

"Business has been crazy, but I'm not complaining. You remember the two part-timers I hired last year to hand out free samples?"

"Yes, of course. Allie and Sidney," Rita said. "Lovely girls."

"They're home from college. I'm pulling them in as backup to help Christina and me."

Christina Diaz had been working at *Patti's Pantry* for the last year and a half after moving to the area from Puerto Rico. She worked five days a week, from Tuesday through Saturday, and managed the social media pages for the bakery. Her live-in boyfriend, Derek, worked with the town and was all she could talk about. Christina was loyal, smart, and mighty opinionated about Patti's love life—or lack thereof.

"I'm glad you have them to help out," Rita said. "The town is already at full capacity."

"If I don't find more permanent staff before next spring, I'll have to pray the *Washington Inn* or *Maison Bleue* has some room on their payrolls for a pastry chef."

Her words made Rita laugh, but it was true: Once the holidays were over, Patti would spend the winter tightening her business plan.

THE ALARM CLOCK WAS SET FOR 4 A.M. PATTI WAS bone-tired and famished. Before bed, she heated up Rita's soup, foolishly burning her mouth with the first spoonful. She ran her tongue across the roof of her mouth and peeled back a layer of skin.

Just then, her phone buzzed with another text alert. It was from Allie, who was scheduled to cover that weekend.

Suddenly, Patti's burnt mouth was the least of her problems.

PARADE WEEKEND

Rita

RITA COULD HARDLY BELIEVE HER WISH HAD COME true: Chase was back! It was as if Christmas morning had arrived early. She hadn't seen him since last year. He seemed taller. Of course, that may have had more to do with her own shrinkage. Yet, it wasn't just his height that surprised her, but the sparks of white hair sprinkled throughout his charcoal facial scruff and crown like stars in a midnight sky. It was one thing to feel the weight of your own years, yet another to see your thirty-six-year-old son bearing some snow on his roof like a gingerbread house—yet another marker of how time was passing. Life was like a runaway train; the longer you stayed on, the faster it went.

"I promise I'll be back as soon as I'm done." Shannon flung her purse over her shoulder, clutching her gift certificate for the day spa.

"Please, take your time. No need to hurry back," Rita said.

Shannon leaned down to Tamra, who was curled like up like a kitten on the loveseat.

"I'll see you soon." She stroked her daughter's red braids which matched her own.

"Have fun, Mom," Miles said, catching both of the women by surprise. Even a mutter was a gift coming from a humorless eleven-year-old boy.

"Thank you, sweetheart. I hope you guys have fun today," Shannon said.

"But not *too* much fun," Tamra said, finishing the punchline she'd heard from her mother over the years.

Rita was glad to see Shannon smiling as she headed out the door. Kids could be complicated, and they held more power over their parents' feelings than they could ever know. How she wished she could tell her sweet daughter-in-law that things would get easier, but she knew just as soon as her grandchildren outgrew the stages they were in, they'd be wheeling toward brand new ones without warning.

"Where's Shannon?" Paul's voice was clipped as he entered the room.

"She left to escape the chains of matrimony and burden of rug rats," Chase said.

He was propped in the armchair closest to the fireplace, thumbing through the weekly *Exit Zero* publication.

"I'm not a rug rat," Miles said.

"Daddy, what's a rug rat?" Tamra said.

"Is there a candlelit walking tour tonight?" Paul asked his mother, ignoring the others.

"Yes, sir. I've got a fresh batch of hot chocolate for our guests," Rita said. "My neighbor will fill in for me while we're at the parade. What's on the agenda for today?"

"I'm taking the kids to Tuckahoe Village for The Santa Express," Paul said.

"Do I have to go?" Miles said. "That's for babies."

"Mom bought these tickets special. Go get ready, please," Paul said.

Miles moved reluctantly up the stairs behind his little sister. Paul rubbed his neck.

"How'd you sleep?" Rita asked.

"My neck feels like steel cables," he said.

"Shannon mentioned there are some issues with Tony?"

"I don't feel like getting into all that right now." Paul's eyes darted around the room.

Rita realized he may not wish to discuss work issues in front of his brother, and it made her miss the days when they could openly review problems as a family.

"It's the stress, bro," Chase said. He set down the magazine and sipped hot chocolate from a large mug. Rita giggled when a glob of whipped cream hung on the tip of his nose. "What?" Chase wiped the cream away with the bandana on his lap. "It's not nice to make fun of your grown son, young lady."

Rita had so desperately missed his good-natured ribbing. She turned to Paul. "Honey, you do seem terribly stressed."

"I'm fine."

If curtness was a sport, Paul could be an Olympian. He called up the stairs to move the children along.

AFTER PAUL LEFT WITH THE KIDS, AN ODD SENSE OF quiet settled into the space. There was a long weekend ahead of them. Rita called the restaurant to see if she could add Chase to their dinner reservation for that evening.

"We're going to *Iccara Italian Bistro* at seven-thirty," Rita said. "You're gonna love it. The fresh ingredients remind me of Nonna's cooking."

"Wow. That good? Cool." Chase paused thoughtfully. "Hey, I think maybe I'll hang back tonight if that's okay," he said.

"Why is that?" Rita said.

"I don't think now's a good time for me to crash the family outing."

Rita didn't like where this was headed.

"Are you not a member of this family anymore?" She put her hands on her hips. "Maybe it would be nice to have dinner with both of my sons for a change."

She wasn't expecting that to come out, but it was how she really felt. Aging had a way of providing the space and encouragement a woman needed to speak up for herself.

"Paul's pretty tense. I don't want to make things worse," he said.

"I simply do not understand why you and your brother can't find a way to get along."

Rita choked up. Her parents had been long gone, and after her sister's passing three years ago, she still hadn't processed being the only one left of her nuclear family—she needed her boys. Her face grew hot with unease. Chase had been home for less than eighteen hours, and there she was standing in the kitchen in her pajamas and slippers, weeping into his shirt.

"It's okay, Mom." He wrapped his arms around her.

She hated losing control of her emotions and resented that she carried all these feelings in the first place. Unfortunately, theirs had not been the warmest of welcomes for Chase. Paul was the Grinch, and Rita, a blubbering Mrs. Claus.

The chimes of the front door rang throughout the lower level of the house. Through the transom, Rita saw Patti standing on the porch, her chestnut brown hair pulled into a bun atop her head. Her face glistened as if she'd been caught in a rainstorm. Her jacket hung from one shoulder and didn't look like it fit well enough to keep her warm. Rita worried for Patti quite a bit. Two years earlier, she had broken things off with her live-in boyfriend and moved to Cape May to make a fresh start. *Patti's Pantry* had been opened shortly thereafter in the face of unprecedented staffing shortages and a disaster of a supply chain.

As Patti entered the house, Rita could see she'd been crying—that made two of them.

"Oh, sweetheart." Rita pulled her in further. "What's the matter?!"

"Why did I think I could do this?" Patti sucked in air between the words. "I can't run a business by myself!"

"We are going to fix whatever is happening." Rita led her to the living room.

"Allie and Sidney were in a car accident. They're okay, but they can't work." Patti resumed her soft weeping. "That's half my staff!"

Rita knew that it would be near impossible to find an extra pair of hands this late in the game. The town was abuzz with tourists, and everything was booked solid. The shops and restaurants were slammed, and most places, if not all, were already pushing maximum capacity with skeletal crews. She wondered if Patti should close up shop for the day, but then, Rita had no idea how much of a hit that would have on her bottom line. This was a dilemma to be sure.

Just as she struggled to find words, Chase sauntered into the room.

"What's up?" he asked, munching on a gingerbread cookie, oblivious to the tension in the room.

"Oh, honey. We're in the middle of a mess right now." Rita scooted across the loveseat and tapped the empty spot next to her.

"What's wrong?" Chase's voice always carried an element of genuine concern—a trait he inherited from Charles.

Rita explained the debacle for Patti who was too upset to speak.

"Sorry to hear. What kind of business is it?" he asked.

"Patti owns the bakery on Washington next to *Whale's Tale*," Rita said.

"A bakery? Why didn't you say so?" Chase said.

Patti and Rita exchanged the side-eye.

"I always work in the cafes of each town I visit," he said. "I donate a portion of my earnings to the local community outreach program for the homeless."

Rita caught a flicker in Patti's eye. She had so much to learn of her son's adventures, but hearing this gave her a glimpse of the Chase she remembered so well. She could still picture that same little boy who held the door and ushered his fellow kindergartners inside, as she watched from the front seat of her car with a soggy tissue.

"What type of work do you do in the cafes?" Rita asked.

"Run the register, take orders, fill coffees. I'm not too bad with a piping bag," Chase said to Patti. "If you got cupcakes that need frosting, I'm your guy."

"I couldn't ask you to do that," Patti said sheepishly.

"You didn't ask. I volunteered. What time should I be there?" Chase asked.

Rita's eyes widened. She nodded to encourage Patti to accept this generous offer.

"Um, well ... Christina and I have things under control for now," Patti said. "In about two hours?"

"Sure thing. I'll jump in the shower and grab something to eat. See you later!" Chase flew up the staircase, skipping every other step.

Rita felt like she was in need of a good, strong pinch to the arm. This last day was like living on a movie set with an ever-evolving script.

"Your son is so nice." Patti dabbed her nose with a tissue.

"He's a good egg," Rita agreed. "Make sure you put him to work. He'll do anything you need. Okay?"

Patti began nervously chewing her cuticles. "I'll pay him."

"Let's not worry about all that right now. We needed a hand, and we got him."

Him. Had Chase not been there to jump in, Rita didn't know what they would have done. This was her big family weekend she'd been planning since buying the house and wouldn't have been able to help Patti. Perhaps Chase was right. Maybe dinner would be less tense if he wasn't there. For now, she decided to leave well enough alone. Surely, there'd be other opportunities for her sons to connect.

"Howdy," Charles said, walking through the front door.

"Hi, Charles," Patti said.

"Nice to see you, Patti," he said.

"How was your walk?" Rita asked.

"Brisk and uneventful," he said. "Where is everyone?"

"Paul and the kids are on The Santa Express. Shannon's at the spa. Chase is in the shower. Patti's having some staffing issues—he's gonna pitch in and help her over at the bakery."

"Good ole Chase. Always lending a hand," Charles said. "If the number of cars I saw crossing the bridge into town this morning is any indication, that bakery of yours is in for one busy night!"

"I know it," Patti said, heading toward the door. "I better get back. Have fun at the parade. And thanks for everything."

"Don't you worry about a thing. Chase is good with his hands, and he follows instructions well," Rita said.

Either she was imagining things, or Patti's rosy cheeks were now crimson. Rita gave her a hug before she left.

"What's been going on in here?" Charles said. "You and Patti both look like you've been crying."

Rita stifled a laugh. She'd never be able to properly explain to Charles the details of what transpired while he was on his walk.

"All is fine now. Like I said, Patti ran into some staffing issues. Thankfully, Chase stepped in," Rita said.

"Speak of the devil ..." Charles said.

Chase was walking down the staircase. Rita was relieved to see he had tidied up and addressed his five o'clock shadow. He slicked his hair back with a green bandana and wore dark blue jeans with a crisp white button-down and brown leather boots.

"Don't you look handsome," she said.

"Looking real sharp, there." Charles nodded in agreement. "Got a date?"

"Yeah, with Mom's friend," Chase joked.

"*Patti's Pantry* is the place. I'll walk you over," Rita said.

"Great. You can join me for a bite before I clock in."

A quick lunch with Chase was just what Rita needed. She hoped to regroup after their awkward conversation from earlier. She also figured the empty house would give Charles an opportunity for a nap before the Christmas parade and dinner.

Stepping outside was like crossing the threshold into a real life winter wonderland. The crowd pulsed with holiday cheer.

How utterly warming to observe the hustle and bustle in between rows of Victorians, with their pitched roofs and wrap-around porches, all tastefully dressed in garland and lights.

Rita thought she might die from charm the moment she heard sleigh bells on the horse-and-carriage ride filled with passengers. Seeing the trolleys reminded her of the time their family took the historic tour when the boys were young. She was convinced their trips to Cape May had ignited Chase's passion for travel and small-town life. No one could convince her there wasn't an inherent sense of magic imbued through the streets.

On their way to lunch, visitors shuffled in and out of shops. One of the neat things about living in a vacation destination was getting to see the tourists enjoying themselves, which sometimes made Rita feel like she was on vacation with them.

"I forgot how Cape May goes all out for the holidays. It's really special here," Chase said.

Delaney's Irish Pub & Grill, previously known as the *Jackson Mountain Cafe*, was located on Washington and Jackson at the highest point of the island, a mere fourteen feet above sea level. The pub featured a *Taste of Ireland* menu with some of the more treasured classics.

They tucked into a booth by the windows. Their server named Molly welcomed them to the restaurant. Rita didn't want to eat too much before dinner, so she ordered the spinach salad.

"Everything sounds good. I think I'll try the corned beef and Swiss," Chase said.

"Good choice," Molly said. "Shall I put in an order of the *Guinness Beer Battered Popcorn Shrimp* to start?"

"Sounds good to me!" Chase said.

Rita closed her menu and drank in the sight of her son. She could hardly believe Chase was in Cape May and sitting across from her. In less than twenty-four hours, everything had changed. When the boys were still in school, she'd bring them to *Friendly's* for waffles and ice-cream after baseball practice. Charles was often held up at the bank, so it was just Rita and the kids. Being at *Delaney's* reminded her of this ancient tradition—yet another Christmas surprise she hadn't expected.

It was refreshing to escape into Chase's world and hear about his new experiences and fascinating travels across America. He was still that same curious and friendly guy who came to life in the company of strangers. As a child, he'd always been interested and engaged with a hunger for exploration. On beach days, when all the kids rode boogie boards and dug trenches in the sand, Chase situated himself by the lifeguard station to ask questions.

He came to know beach patrol so well that they gave him his very own T-shirt. Of course, he asked if they had one for his brother too. Chase was always looking out for Paul—even if Paul didn't know it. Rita took a photograph of them wearing the shirts in front of a red Cape May rescue boat surrounded by lifeguards. She had it framed in one of the guest rooms. Tamra had taken a particular liking to the framed photographs of her daddy and uncle. The boys' shared excitement from that day is what stuck out most for Rita. If only she could help them find a way back to each other.

"I really want to thank you for helping Patti out. She's become a dear friend."

"Sure thing. She seems nice," Chase said.

"She is, and a whole lot more." Rita smiled. "Before you were born, your Aunt Gina was close with Patti's mother."

"Didn't you guys live in Wildwood before moving to Pennsylvania?" he asked.

"That's right. Grandpa got a job transfer once I started middle school. Aunt Gina was already heading off to college by then. Anyway, it's good to have you back home, kiddo. I know this isn't the house you grew up in."

"Mom, home will always be wherever you and Dad are."

When they approached the bakery, a few custom-ers were waiting in line. Patti was filling four large to-go cups. She looked up as they approached.

"Oh, hi," she said. "Thanks for coming."

"Thanks for saying yes." The conspiratorial twinkle in Chase's eye was reminiscent of Santa Claus.

Patti handed him a white apron with *Patti's Pantry* em-broidered on the front. Rita overheard one customer men-tion the folks who set out their beach chairs to secure seating along the parade's route at 3 p.m. the day before—the parade was serious business for most locals and returning guests.

Rita waved goodbye and slipped out the door, unable to resist watching them through the window. These two had their work cut out for them. Anyone observing Patti in action could clearly see she was a professionally trained chef. Rita marveled at the gals from the younger generations who embraced their independence. Many seemed driven to find themselves and discover their talents before committing to a lifelong partner.

Chase had somehow dunked his hands in flour, as a cloud of white powder coated his face, hair, and the front of his apron. Patti was still laughing as she turned on her heels to help the next customer. What a relief it was to see her in better spirits.

Rita had to admit, seeing the kids working side by side, they could certainly pass for a couple.

The thought sparked a butterfly dance in her belly.

PARADE WEEKEND

Paul

HIS BROTHER'S UNEXPECTED DROP-IN WAS A COMPLETE disruption. And, of course, Paul was the only one with that opinion. It was embarrassing how the whole family gushed over Chase. He half expected it from his mother and the kids, but even Dad and Shannon carried on like he was a soldier returning from combat. Paul thought perhaps he should disappear for a while. Maybe his family would fuss over him when he returned. The idea made him scoff as he exited the Garden State Parkway.

"Daddy, are we almost there?" Tamra said from the backseat.

"Just about," Paul said.

"Uncle Chase said he's gonna take us roller skating the day after Christmas," Tamra said.

Paul tightened his grip on the steering wheel. Now his brother was staying until Christmas? He wondered how long this unexpected visit was going to last.

"I'm not going. Roller skating is for babies," Miles said.

"I told you to knock it off with the baby stuff." Paul opened his mouth to stretch the muscles of his jaw. He'd been grinding again at night.

They finally arrived at Tuckahoe Village in Upper Township for The Santa Express. The train's cabin was decked out with garland and bells. Tamra was fascinated by the crew members dressed as elves and swung her legs to and fro excitedly. She was a good-natured little girl—and looking more like her mother every day. Miles, on the other hand, scowled out the window with his arms folded across his chest. The five years between the kids had finally caught up. Lumping activities for them to share was no longer working—he would have to break it to Shannon.

Paul's phone vibrated in his pocket. There was an email from the office assistant. Apparently, there was a problem with the last job Paul did before he left for Cape May. He was being asked to report back on the job site right away on Monday morning. Unfortunately, he was already scheduled to finish up another ongoing job first thing on Monday; Paul would have to call the office and have them reschedule. Normally, he would just text Tony, but ever since Ralph's visit—which still had not been mentioned—Paul was keeping his distance. After the holidays were over, he'd buck up the courage for a heart-to-heart. For now, he'd let Tony enjoy this time with his family and try not to have a meltdown.

As Paul bit into his turkey sandwich, a jolt of pain coursed through his jaw muscles that were now tender to the touch. He took small, careful bites and sloshed the food around with his tongue.

"When is this gonna be over?" Miles whined.

Paul tried to swallow the food in his mouth and wound up biting down on his tongue, hard.

"Dammit!" Paul slammed the rest of his sandwich onto the table. "Will you cut me a break?"

Tamra's pink lemonade spilled across the table. She jutted out her bottom lip, which started to quiver.

All heads turned. Suddenly, Paul and the kids were the main attraction in the train car. Miles straightened his posture and grabbed a wad of napkins to clean up the mess. It was a good thing Shannon wasn't there to witness this display. He had promised her he'd keep his frustration levels in-check.

"I'm sorry, baby." Paul rubbed Tamra's back to soothe her.

Once they were back on the road, an eerie silence hung in the car like dense smog. He knew he frightened and embarrassed the children and felt like garbage for it. From the rearview mirror, he saw Miles show Tamra something on his iPad. Both kids started giggling.

"What's going on?" Paul asked.

The two communicated in hushed voices followed by more laughter.

"Does anyone wanna let me in on the joke?" Paul said.

"It's Uncle Chase," Tamra said.

Again with Uncle Chase?

"It's a clip from last summer when he was traveling through New Mexico," Miles said.

For once, Paul kept any snide remarks to himself, but it stung to know that the smiles on his kids' faces were because his brother had put them there.

Given the heavy traffic in town, it was a Christmas miracle that Paul found a parking spot just a few blocks from his parents' house. He and Miles followed closely behind Tamra, who waved her arms as if dancing.

"Listen!" she said. "It sounds so pretty."

As they drew closer to the house, they could see there were carolers on the front porch singing "The First Noel". Even Paul had to admit, the carolers really raised the bar. He gave them a friendly wave and followed the kids inside the house.

Shannon sauntered down the hallway, glowing from her treatment at the day spa.

"You look rested. How was it?" Paul asked.

"Soooo good. Totally relaxing." She stretched her arms out and squeezed her eyes shut. Her red hair was luminous, cascading like a waterfall over her shoulders. She dazzled him. That was one thing that could never change.

"Where are my parents?" he asked.

"Rita's getting washed up for dinner. Charles is napping in the den."

"And my brother?"

"I'm not really sure. I think he's helping Patti over at the bakery."

"Are you serious?" he asked.

Chase was in town for less than twenty-four hours and was already playing hero for Patti the baker.

"How was The Santa Express? Tamra was bouncing when I saw her," Shannon said.

"Yeah, she was excited." Paul shrugged. "You know how she gets."

"I'm afraid to ask about Miles. He just grunted when I saw him. He's probably getting too old for that sort of thing," she said.

"Not probably. He's over it," Paul said.

"I'm sorry." Shannon squeezed his shoulder. "Did you at least enjoy it?"

"Yeah ..." He really didn't want to tell her but knew it was the right thing to do. It would be worse if she heard it from one of the kids first. "I bit my tongue."

"About what?" Shannon said.

"No, I literally bit my tongue. My jaw is killing me ... I can hardly chew, and I bit my friggin' tongue. I slammed the sandwich down."

Her sullen expression twisted his gut.

"Miles was wearing on me. He can be a real pain in the ass," Paul insisted.

"You don't think I know that? He's eleven. Of course he's a pain in the ass," Shannon said.

"He kept complaining about being there. I say the same things over and over. The money was already spent. I didn't want to waste the tickets."

Shannon smiled sadly.

"You did waste the tickets, Paul."

CAPE MAY, NJ

Parade Weekend

Patti

PATTI LOCKED THE DOOR AS THE LAST CUSTOMER EXITed the bakery. The crowd that night was unprecedented. She, Christina, and Chase had been on their feet for hours. After running on fumes for days, Patti was ready to drop.

"Great teamwork," Chase said.

He raised both hands to give Patti and Christina high fives.

"We did it!" Christina said.

"Thanks for jumping in at the last minute," Patti said.

Chase nodded humbly and turned his back to start washing the mixing bowls and measuring cups piled in the sink.

"Be right back. I have to check the freezer," Patti said.

Replenishing inventory was of constant concern in her world. Even with adequate assistance, there were some things only Patti could do.

According to the register tally, that night was the highest in sales for *Patti's Pantry* to date. The freezer had just enough stock to see them through Sunday.

Christina entered the back room.

"Okay, Mama. He is seriously cute. And *really* sweet." She was gushing.

"Who? Derek?" Patti sighed. "Yes, Derek is the best. You picked a good one."

"You know who I mean. *Chase* ..." Christina dragged out his name.

"He's cool," Patti replied.

"He's more than cool." Christina hunched over the laptop on the desk. Her shiny black hair fanned out over her bony shoulders.

"What are you up to?" Patti said.

Chase's website popped up on the screen.

"You can't ignore Prince Charming just because he's your friend's son," Christina said.

"You've watched one too many Disney movies, girlfriend," Patti scoffed.

"We don't get Disney in the Caribbean," Christina teased. "This one is a real do-gooder. And I don't see any sign of a lady friend on his social media."

"You and your one-track mind." Patti was amused. "You can't go around trying to fix me up with every cute guy who breezes through town. Speaking of, please go back out front and help him clean while I straighten up back here. And try to behave yourself. Pretty please."

Ever since Christina met Derek, she was on a mission to find Patti a boyfriend. It wasn't that Patti didn't want one. Of course, it would be nice to have someone to slather her back with aloe during a post-beach dinner for two at *Taco Caballito*, but she was just starting to build on this next part of her dream. Her plate was full, as were her hands. Plus, Patti doubted she was Chase's type. She figured he preferred women who were more ... *petite*.

Chase's site was still up on the screen. There was a photograph of him on the deck of the Cape May-Lewes Ferry. Patti scanned the tabs across the top of the screen: *Photo Gallery*; *You Tube*; *Furry Friends*; *Community Outreach*; *Chasing the Dream*. Patti clicked on the last tab. The entries went back more than five years. The latest reel was posted at 10 p.m. last night.

"Yo! Yo! Yo! Season's greetings, friends, followers, and randoms. I'm touching base tonight from a place which is close to my heart: Cape May, New Jersey. If so inclined, pull up a map, and you'll see it's located at the tippy-end of the state where the Atlantic Ocean meets the Delaware Bay. When we were kids, our parents took us here for summers and holidays. The town was dubbed *America's First Seaside Resort*. We learned how to boogie board and surf right here on these beaches."

The next frame showed a sprawling photo of the Abernathy's home.

"At the beginning of this year, my folks bought a one-hundred-and-fifty-year-old Victorian. I admit I thought they lost their minds, but it turned out to be a pretty cool thing. The house is featured on one of the Christmas tours. You guys need to add Cape May to your travel bucket lists. It's like stepping back in time with the gaslit lampposts and horse-drawn carriages. You food buffs will feast here. The shopping is bar none. Really, the production these towns-people pull off for the holiday season is nothing short of Herculean. It's even more special than I remember. And to think the parade is funded by donations and volunteers. You'll find a link at the bottom of this video for *Borough Hall of West Cape May*, if anyone is interested in making a modest donation. Even one dollar helps and is much appreciated."

This frame was of Chase walking the Washington Mall. Unbelievably, the *Patti's Pantry* sign was in the background as he spoke.

"You know my message is all about how perspective can shift and mutate over time. How the old becomes new again with fresh eyes. Find ways to hit the pause button this holiday season and connect to your roots if you can. Stay open. Make time for a chat with a stranger at the local coffee shop. Allow yourself to get lost along the way. Maybe you'll find an even better view than you imagined."

Chase looked right into the camera as he delivered the last lines. A halo of light surrounded him and bounced off his sunglasses in all directions.

Patti closed the laptop. She was intrigued. He did seem pretty great, if a little quirky. She could also see why Rita's sons weren't all that close. When Patti first met Paul, he was cordial enough, but removed, whereas Chase was approachable in a way of that made people feel like they mattered.

She turned off the overhead lights and headed to the front. Suddenly, Patti became self-conscious for having just been on Chase's website. It was a creepy thing to do, but Christina put her up to it.

He seemed to be quite comfortable sitting at one of the front tables with a cup of coffee, looking at a sign Patti had posted for the *Cape May Food Closet*.

"I'd like to help," he said.

"There's a wish list on Amazon of items they need," she said.

"I like to find out what makes a community tick and how to help those less fortunate."

"It sounds like you've done a lot of traveling," Patti said.

"I guess my mom talks a lot about us. It's been fun. I've seen new places, made some money from YouTube views and a few sponsorships. I'm ready for what's next." Chase chuckled.

"What's funny?"

"I heard my sister-in-law Shannon talking to Mom the other day. She said she was ready for her next chapter. I relate to her more than my own brother."

Patti had so many questions, but nothing seemed appropriate in that moment.

"I can think of times in my life when I knew I reached a crossroads and it was time to start something new," she said.

"Like this bakery?" Chase asked.

"I worked for the previous owner after graduation," she said. "I knew I didn't want to sling coffee and buttered rolls for the rest of my life, but I needed to be as close to living the dream as possible. Here I am."

"Makes sense to me. You needed hands-on experience. The best way to learn is from the people who are doing it better than you or are in the place you're trying to get to. You're smart."

Patti basked for a moment in the compliment.

"I'd love to hear how a girl from Bucks County came to own a bakery in the heart of Cape May," Chase said.

"Well, you know, my mom is originally from Wildwood. Me and my sister spent our summers on Morey's Pier. I guess you could say I've had a lifelong affinity for the area."

"That's right. My mother reminded me that my aunt and your mom were friends when our family still lived here. That's crazy."

"Not many degrees of separation in Cape May County," Patti said.

"So, why baking?" he asked.

Patti explained her culinary pursuits began when her Great Aunt Mary visited for Christmas. Uncle Jim had just died. Since the couple never had any children, and with most of the family gone, Mary would have been all alone for the holidays. For the next eight years, she camped out on the Kelleys' pullout sofa for a weeklong Christmas celebration.

Upon arrival, Aunt Mary would request a trip to the supermarket for her long list of baking supplies. Patti loved to tag along and buckled herself in to the back of her mother's minivan. Her aunt methodically scanned prices and ingredients, as the shopping cart slowly filled. They'd return from the market and head straight for the kitchen. Aunt Mary was the first to tie an apron around Patti; she showed her how to set a proper workstation with mixing bowls, parchment paper, rolling pins, and flour.

Patti's time with her aunt turned out to be a lifelong gift. Aunt Mary loved Christmastime and good food and showed Patti how to love them, too. As an adult, the magic of the season dwindled with time, but Patti still carried a piece of her aunt's splendor throughout the year. With every batter she stirred, every dough she pounded, Patti could feel her dear Aunt Mary abiding. She wished she could thank her for letting a curious little kid hang around, and for clearing the path to the big-girl dreams inside her.

"I usually pay Christina on Fridays. Would you mind waiting until then?" Patti asked.

"It was a favor." Chase dismissed the thought with a hand. "You don't have to pay me."

"It was a big favor, and you saved my butt tonight. I would have ended up drowning myself in the cappuccino machine, and I can almost bet Christina would have been cursing in Spanish under her breath and threatening to spray impatient customers with whipped cream. Seriously, you deserve to get paid for your time."

"How about dinner instead?"

Patti recognized the flicker in his eyes from the video.

"Dinner?"

"Dinner. You and me," he said. "You pick the time and place."

Patti looked down at her hands. There were dried pieces of dough caked beneath her fingernails. The backs of her tired and heavy legs glued her to the chair. She was worn, dehydrated, and needed about a week of rest.

Attention from guys—especially the super cute ones—had always been a trap for her. They usually ended up liking her just as a friend. For a million reasons, she should say no. Then, she thought of Rita; her only reason to say yes.

Patti tucked a few loose strands of hair behind one ear. Her eyes met his.

"You're on."

PARADE WEEKEND

Rita

"DOES PATTI HAVE A BOYFRIEND?"

Shannon spoke under her breath and slid her chair closer to Rita's so no one at the table would hear their conversation.

"Not that I'm aware of." Rita leaned in.

"Are you thinking what I'm thinking?" Shannon looked like she was storing chestnuts in those spirited Irish cheeks.

"Maybe we'll pop by the bakery on the way home. For all we know they could need something." Rita winked.

"Good plan."

Having Shannon at dinner was a comfort, considering how tense the rest of the family was. Since Paul and the kids returned from The Santa Express, Miles had grown especially distant. He wouldn't make eye contact with anyone at the table and hypnotically rolled a cherry tomato drenched in balsamic dressing across his salad plate. Rita feared her son's dark moods were getting the best of him and starting to affect the other family members. She certainly didn't want to put a damper on the evening, but she was going to have to follow up with Paul about his work situation with Tony when the family wasn't around.

After dinner, the Abernathy family began their walk back to the house. As the energy from the day's parade died down, a stillness settled over the town like a blanket of fresh snow. It was a marvel to see the area through Shannon's eyes. Rita knew her daughter-in-law would love it just as much as she had.

"I see what you mean about the magic," Shannon said. "It's like being on a movie set or something."

"Not you, too," Charles said.

"But it's true!" Shannon said.

She went on to explain the luxurious massage she'd had called *Tension Tamer* at the *Cape May Day Spa* which had miraculously cured the pain in her shoulder and eased her headache.

"I just can't get over the stores. It's a shopper's paradise," Shannon said.

Paul muttered under his breath.

"It's something, isn't it?" Rita said.

She wanted Shannon to experience all the special nuances of the town. On their way to dinner, they stopped in at the *Cape Atlantic Book Company* to say hello to Rita's friend Mary Ann, who was known for her supersized hugs and thoughtful book recommendations. Shannon left with a novel by a local author and one on the history of *The Cape May Sentinel* for Paul.

"Who wants to go see Uncle Chase?" Rita said, knowing full-well that would perk the kids right up.

Miles and Tamra shouted, "Me!" at the same time.

Within minutes, the wooden sign for *Patti's Pantry* came into focus. The dim lights showcased a silhouette of two bodies tucked into the front cafe booth nearest to the front window.

Charles stifled a yawn.

"I'm gonna head back to the house with Dad," Paul said.

Charles looked ragged. Eventually, Rita would have to find more creative ways for her sons to be together than a drive-by at the end of an exhausting day for everyone.

"Is Uncle Chase in there?" Tamra pointed.

Rita leaned down and kissed the forehead of her mini-Shannon. It struck her that they had reached the stage of life where her and Charles' bedtime was more pressing than their granddaughter's.

"I see him!" It was the most Miles said all night. He knocked on the door.

Chase sprang to his feet. He smiled when he recognized his nephew and unlocked the door.

"The boss says you may enter even though we're closed."

"Uncle Chase!"

Chase opened his arms. Both kids gravitated to his fun-loving, youthful energy.

"So, how'd it go?" Rita asked.

"I'm pretty sure it was our biggest night yet," Patti said.

Rita was thrilled that Chase had been there to help.

"Really?" Chase moved in closer to Patti and touched her on the shoulders.

"Really," she said, looking up at him.

Rita knew she was tired, but surely her mind wasn't playing tricks this time—Patti and Chase seemed right at home with each other.

"I'm proud of you both." Rita wasn't sure if they heard her, as they didn't take their eyes off each other.

The kids were hopped up on sugar from dessert and clearly overtired, and it was well past Rita's bedtime.

"Here, take these." Patti handed Shannon a bakery bag. "We had some left over. They make for a yummy breakfast."

Shannon peeked inside the bag and held it against her chest. "Oh, thank you so much, Patti!"

Rita embraced Chase and spoke into his ear. "Thank you, sweetheart."

"Of course," he said softly. "I'm gonna help Patti lock up and walk her home."

Rita held the side of his smooth face with her hand. "Ever the gentleman," she said. Both of her sons had grown into kind-hearted men—it was one of her greatest life accomplishments.

As they walked away from the bakery, Shannon huddled up to Rita.

"They are *so* cute together!"

"Yes, they are." Rita raised an eyebrow with cautious optimism.

They followed the neat rows of homes, festooned in a kaleidoscope of lights. As they turned the corner, the Victorian came into view. Through the picture window, Rita could see the Christmas tree still lit. Charles sat comfortably in his chair as Paul stoked the fire. At long last, all the members of their family were in the same town.

The Abernathy family's first Cape May Christmas had officially begun.

DECEMBER 6TH

Paul

THE CHEERFUL DECORATIONS OF THEIR FESTIVE HOME decor belied the silenced tension between Paul and Shannon. He hadn't made things right with her after losing his temper with Miles on their visit to Cape May, as the craze of the holiday season amped up the already chaotic nature of their family life.

Every morning, Shannon beat the alarm and jumped on her laptop before waking the kids for breakfast. Between her new skincare side gig, Christmas shopping, and carpools for play rehearsals, there never seemed to be a good time for a serious talk. They were trapped in a pattern of feigned politeness, and Paul had no idea how to fix it.

Tony hadn't been in the office, and when he was, Paul seemed to just miss him. Then, an uninvited guest had been making appearances at the office. Tony's sister's son, who Paul affectionately referred to as *The Nephew*, had been squatting in the storage area with his computer. Between the nephew's presence in the office and Ralph Grayhall's visit a few weeks back, Paul was more confused than ever. Was Tony planning on selling? And if so, to whom? Grayhall? Or his nephew?

The rumor mill thrived in the trades. The building inspectors, property managers, and school supers were the "water cooler" pals of Paul's workweek.

Earlier that day, he had a conversation with Skip, the super at the middle school Miles attended.

"How's old man Tony doing?" Skip asked.

"He's doing all right," Paul said.

"Is he getting ready to hang up the plunger, or what?" Skip laughed at his own bad joke.

"I don't know anything."

"How 'bout that. You're his main guy. Thought you knew it all," Skip said.

"Guess not."

"How long you been there now?"

"It'll be sixteen years in June." Even Paul could hardly believe it.

"Oh, man. Did Tony snatch you from nursery school or something?" Skip laughed at his second bad joke, but his remarks stuck.

The heavy conversations Paul needed to have with his wife and his boss—only the two most important people in his life—shadowed his every thought like a storm cloud.

He'd have to find a way to make it through the holidays without burning a hole in his stomach.

One afternoon in between jobs, Paul parked along the Black Horse Pike to scarf down a sandwich in his truck. His phone rang. It was his mother. Rita wasn't one to bother her kids during the workday. He grabbed it immediately.

"Dad and I are fine, sweetheart," she said. "I'm calling to check in on you."

Paul had a feeling this was coming. His mother tried to be direct in her communication, where he and his father failed miserably. He was still embarrassed over his behavior on Thanksgiving and was glad she didn't know about his outburst in front of the kids on The Santa Express.

"I'm very happy your brother is home. I know you two have your differences, but it is Christmastime and would be nice if you could try and mend fences."

"Chase is a glutton for attention, and everyone feeds into him," Paul said.

"I don't think that's true," she said. "His business requires him to travel and talk to people. Sharing his discoveries online is part of the job. He was always a curious and friendly child."

Paul gritted his teeth. He didn't feel like hearing his mother's soupy nostalgia about what a wonder her firstborn was. He knew what his brother was like and didn't need his mother weighing in with her own partiality.

"What is happening with Tony?" Rita asked.

He couldn't believe he had to talk about this crap in the middle of his workday.

"Grayhall's truck was parked outside his office one Saturday," Paul said.

"As in Ralph Grayhall? Your biggest competitor?"

"The very one," he said. "Tony still hasn't mentioned anything about it to me."

"That's odd. You and Tony are so close."

Paul grunted. "Yeah, I don't know ..."

"Darling, you've been working together for so long. You've been a loyal and steadfast right-hand to Tony. He appreciates that. I know he does."

Her words sparked a lump in Paul's throat. He wanted to cry, which infuriated him. He would not lose it in front of his mother like a weak little baby.

"I really think you should come right out and ask him what he is planning," Rita said. "You have a right to know."

Before they hung up, Paul told her he would think it over and let her suggestion simmer until he figured out his next move.

That evening, he found Shannon camped out in the family room. She looked like a college student on the beanbag chair with her laptop. Papers and notebooks covered the futon and coffee table. It made Paul feel bad that they were still living in their starter home. Shannon never pushed or complained, but it ate away at his self-confidence to not be able to provide a proper home office space for his wife.

Shannon appeared content, but also like she could use a good night's rest. Her face was shiny from lotion. The whole room smelled like lavender and cucumber. Her hair was still damp from her shower, turning it an elegant red. Paul had an impulsive urge to kiss his beautiful wife and obliterate this invisible wall between them—he should have.

DECEMBER 6TH

Patti

"HE'S CLEARLY INTERESTED IN YOU, HONEY. WHY ELSE does he stop by twice a day?" Christina said.

Chase Abernathy had become a regular at the bakery. Most of their regulars stopped in just once a day, but not Chase. He showed first thing every morning and then again in the afternoon. Naturally, Christina had drawn her own conclusions.

"The man appreciates professional-grade coffee and quality baked goods. He's not coming here for this."

Patti turned around and slapped herself on the butt using both hands which made Christina guffaw just as Chase walked in.

"Am I interrupting something?" he asked, looking her over in a dramatic fashion.

Christina was giddier than ever. Patti wanted to shrivel up and die. How did she always manage to look like a complete goofball?

"I made some of that mulled wine I was telling you about," Chase said, pointing to the glass jug in his hand. "I thought it would pair well with our dinner tonight."

Patti shifted on her feet.

"Mulled wine? I don't think I ever heard of this before," Christina said.

"It's a pretty seasonal drink. I imagine it's not too popular in the tropics," he said. "I've got the recipe up on my website."

"I'll be checking that out." Christina smiled wickedly.

Of course you will be, Patti thought.

"I'll be out in a few minutes." Patti headed to the back office.

She had trouble sleeping in the days leading up to their dinner. Even her top-grade coffee wasn't playing nice with her stomach lately. She was totally out of practice when it came to guys—especially ones who were equal parts handsome, fun, and kind. She hadn't dated anyone seriously since her breakup, and her last date, which was over a year ago, was totally unmemorable. Not that this was a date. This was simply a pay-back.

As Patti peered into the small compact mirror, it reminded her of culinary school when the crew would all head out for drinks to blow off steam after class. She had come a long way since those days and owned a bakery now. Surely, she could handle something as simple as having dinner with Rita's son.

She took a deep breath and entered the front of the bakery where Chase was waiting with a grin.

THEY DECIDED ON *GRANA BYOB* ON SOUTH BROADWAY in West Cape May where *Godmother's Restaurant* used to be. The new restaurant was started by renowned Chef Carl Messick after he left a decade tenure at *Peter Shields Inn*.

Chase's mulled wine was a burnt red-orange. Cinnamon and clove wafted from their mugs. A burst of honey left a smooth finish to the tartness.

"Tell me how it works again with the coasties who come in for free coffee," Chase said.

Patti explained the fund set up for the cadets on the coast-guard base. Locals and visitors alike could contribute money so the coasties could receive complimentary coffees and treats.

"It's so special that you do that," he said.

"I got the idea from *Coffee Tyme*. They're the generous ones," said Patti.

Chase examined the Band-Aid around her index finger. "Did our baker sustain a baking injury?"

"I cut myself wrapping presents for the kids," Patti said.

"The kids?"

"There's a woman in Rio Grande who sends me a wish list every year for foster children in the area. I usually pick a couple of families or one large one," she said.

Chase considered this. "How old are they?"

"Anywhere from newborn to seventeen. The teens mostly want gift cards, which is easy enough. For the babies, I look for onesies, teething rings, and rattles. It's the five- to fourteen-year-olds who are the most fun to shop for. I get to learn about the latest toys, games, and kiddie fashion."

"Do they ever find out that you are the angel behind all those gifts?" Chase asked, topping off their mulled wines.

"What do you mean?" Patti said. "The presents are from Santa Claus." She smiled. "I feel like everyone should try and hold on to that magic for as long as possible."

"I couldn't agree more."

"I like knowing the less fortunate kids in the area will have something to open on Christmas morning like I always did," she added.

Chase searched her face for a beat.

"I'd like to adopt one of the families," he said.

Patti promised to send the contact information. Even if all of the families had been accounted for, there was always an urgent community need for clothing, food, and provisions—especially this time of year.

"Is it too cold for a walk on the promenade?" Chase asked as he pulled up to the curb in front of Patti's apartment.

"I have an early morning," she said.

"Rain check, then. I really enjoyed tonight."

"Thank you for helping me out last week," she said.

"You're never gonna let that go, are you?"

"I will now."

PATTI KNEW CHRISTINA WOULD YELL AT HER FOR NOT taking that walk with Chase, but it was already too late. As much as she liked the guy, she was conflicted. He wasn't just some hot random stranger, he was Rita's son, and she didn't want anything to get in the way of their friendship.

Patti needed a distraction and found herself right back on Chase's website, mindlessly scrolling.

There was another entry posted earlier that morning with a link: *What makes Cape May so special?* Images of the town flashed across the screen before Chase started speaking.

"I'm not even going to make you wait. I will tell you right here and now, it is the people of Cape May that make the town so special. An extraordinary effort is made to preserve the historical integrity of this small city."

The *Patti's Pantry* sign came into full view with customers coming and going. Patti sipped water and continued to listen, wondering when he recorded this, because clearly, she and Christina had both missed it.

"For those of my followers who are smart enough to have already added Cape May to your travel dockets, be sure to stop in and spread some love to my friends over at *Patti's Pantry*. I had the great fortune of helping out at this cool spot on the night of the Christmas parade, and the owner hasn't stopped thanking me.

"Patti Kelley is a professional pastry chef and the mastermind behind this bakery. Trust me on this: Her croissants will change your life for the better. This is a shining example of what coming home should taste like."

The screen shifted to the new *Cape May Point Science Center* at the tip of the island.

"Bob Mullock saved this historic building from demolition in 2021. It was previously known as *Saint Mary by the Sea*. The 38,000-square-foot Victorian structure began as the *Shoreham Hotel*. Throughout the centuries, it served as a refuge for enslaved people seeking freedom after crossing the water from Delaware, as well as a hospital. Since 1909, it was a retreat for the *Sisters of Saint Joseph*, before Mullock—along with his team of experts and conservationists—stepped in."

Chase's reel ended with an image of *The Sentinel* on *Cape May Point State Park* with Christmas instrumental music in the background. Patti paused the video and sat in stillness to absorb all she had seen and heard.

And then the phone rang. It was Christina. Even for her, it was too late to be calling just to hear about Patti's dinner with Chase—something was wrong.

"Are you okay? What happened?"

"Chica, my phone is blowing up!" Christina was more excited than usual.

"What do you mean?"

"Orders are coming in from all over the country!"

"What? Orders for what?" Patti was perplexed.

"For your croissant assortment! Text alerts are pouring in from our website and social media pages!"

Patti felt like someone had just dumped a bucket of ice water over her head.

Christina continued. "Dios mío! Now they're all over our Instagram page!"

Patti's eyes drifted back to her computer. She stared at Chase's image which was now frozen on her screen.

Who the heck are you, Chase Abernathy?

DECEMBER 11TH

Rita

CHASE HAD ALWAYS BEEN AN EARLY RISER. HE explained the importance of exploring a town in the quiet morning hours in order to mingle with locals who provided a wellspring of knowledge and information.

One morning, Rita caught him at the kitchen table before he left the house. An interesting phenomenon had taken place in her recycling bin—there was an overflow of to-go coffee cups from *Patti's Pantry*.

"How did your dinner go with Patti?" she asked.

"I really enjoy her company." He grinned. "We have a lot in common."

Yes, you do, she thought. One of the first things that struck her about Patti was her good heart and sense of community—same as Chase's.

"So …" Rita took her seat at the kitchen table, an indication it was time for a sit-down.

Chase sat across from her, tenting his hands on the table.

"You seem to have taken a liking to bakery coffee."

She couldn't resist. Maybe Chase was old enough to make decisions for his own life, but this involved Patti, and she had a right to know.

"Yes, I do." Chase smiled coyly. His Scottish roots poked through on his ruddy skin.

"I care a great deal for that young lady, you know," Rita said.

"So do I," he said. "She's pretty special."

"Life can get tricky. It's good to have a plan," she said.

"Mom, I'm thirty-six years old. I know all about life's tricks."

"You're thirty-*what*? How can that be? I just turned forty-seven."

Chase planned on spending the rest of the year in Cape May. Naturally, Rita loved having him there, and Charles certainly didn't mind the extra set of hands for the firewood. Chase was certainly welcome to stay for as long as he liked.

Rita vowed not to meddle in her son's love life, but if given the chance, she'd remind him that sometimes you can be searching for your glasses when they're already sitting right on top of your head.

"ANY NEWS ON OUR LOVEBIRDS?"

Shannon had been calling more often under the guise of checking in on the Chase and Patti situation. Rita soon realized her daughter-in-law was in need of some emotional support. They'd speak during the day when Paul was at work and the kids were at school.

"Let's just say my recycling bin is a tell-all," Rita said.

She explained the new collection of coffee cups that had turned up from the bakery.

"Sounds like he is stopping in there pretty often," Shannon said.

"If often is twice a day, then yes."

"This is so exciting!"

It was fun playing matchmaker, but Rita knew they had more important things to discuss.

"How is the skincare business going?" she asked.

"Things are going okay. I'm *really* tired, but also *really* happy," Shannon said.

"Kind of like having a newborn. Those first few months are both exhausting and exhilarating," Rita said.

"Exactly. You're so good at analogies. Must be the librarian in you."

She knew Shannon was being sincere, but she somehow always got Rita to laugh at herself.

"Miles has been quiet. Other than driving him all over the place and eating tons of food, he doesn't require much. Tamra has been especially clingy," Shannon said. "Hopefully it's just a phase."

Rita was a boy mom, as they said these days, and out of her league here. When it came to little girls, she only knew how to play Grammi.

"How has Paul been with all the work stress? Any more news on Tony?"

Rita thought it would be best not to mention her phone call to Paul, since he had leveled with her about his feelings on Chase. She certainly didn't want to say or do anything that would cause more upset or strain between her sons.

"I don't really know. We've been staying out of each other's way ever since the parade weekend ..." Shannon cut herself off.

"What happened on parade weekend?" Rita asked.

"It's nothing, really. Paul had a little temper flare-up when he took the kids to The Santa Express."

Rita remembered the tension that day after Paul and the kids had returned from their excursion.

"I'm sorry to hear this, Shannon."

"It's okay. We're both too stressed to even argue, so we're not really speaking."

Rita could relate. Shannon and Paul sounded a lot like her and Charles.

"You both have a lot of spinning tops and two kids to raise. Life can certainly overwhelm."

"How'd you do it, Rita?"

Shannon could be so achingly dear.

"I don't even know. There was always something to be done, no matter where I looked. As soon as I sat down, I was beckoned by Charles, one of the boys, or my own racing mind. I'd fall into bed at the end of the day, wishing I could sleep for days and days."

"You are describing my life," Shannon said.

Well, what do ya know, Rita thought.

She made a mental note to brainstorm with Mary Ann from the bookstore to find some self-help books to guide and inspire Shannon in her new business venture. Rita believed the best way to show your love for someone was with the perfect book recommendation.

"Remember you asked me what I want for Christmas?" Rita asked.

"Yes. Please, tell me," Shannon said.

"I want my sons to end this cold war or whatever is going on between them. It would be nice if we could find ways to get them together."

"It's too bad we won't see Chase again until Christmas," Shannon said.

"Mommy?"

Rita could hear Tamra stirring in the background.

"Excuse me, sweetheart, Mommy's on an important call," Shannon said.

"But, I have something to tell you," Tamra said.

Rita's granddaughter still had that impossibly precious baby-girl voice. She dreaded the day it would be gone.

"What is it, honey?" Shannon said.

"Is Uncle Chase coming to my play next week?" Tamra asked.

"Oh. We will have to ask—" Shannon said.

"Tell her yes!" Rita interjected. "Tell her Uncle Chase is coming with Grandpa and Grammi!"

"Okay." Shannon lowered her voice. "But, how will we make them talk?"

"I don't know yet. Maybe we should ask the six-year-old."

The women shared a chuckle, as Rita's mind wheeled with possibilities.

PAUL AND SHANNON'S SITUATION HAD STAYED WITH Rita. It conjured a lot of old—and bad—memories. Charles had enjoyed a long, illustrious career at the bank. But many years earlier, there was some talk of a merger which threatened his position as branch manager. He'd built walls around himself, same as Paul, while Rita frantically sought ways to trim their household spending. Her part-time job at the library wasn't enough to sustain them financially. It was not only a lonely and scary time in her life, but also within her marriage. There were times when her husband's brooding was the loudest thing in their home with a three- and five-year old.

Rita had blocked out that time in her life, but spending these last few weeks talking to Shannon brought back unpleasant memories. She approached Charles one night on the subject, after he returned from chopping firewood.

"I'd like you to speak to your son," she said, hoping he'd have more luck with Paul.

"Which one and about what?" Charles asked.

"Shannon mentioned that Paul is worried about losing his job."

"I thought his job with Tony was a sure thing."

"Since when is anything in life a sure thing? You should know that better than anyone."

Charles grew somber. Rita knew to tread lightly on this delicate terrain. Those couple of years had been a bleak time for them.

"I can't force a man to talk about something that he doesn't want to," he said.

"I understand that, but I think reminding him that you are a sounding board could help some."

"I'll give him a call tomorrow."

In the past, Rita wouldn't have believed him, but surprisingly, Charles followed through.

The next night after supper, he retreated to his study and called Paul. Rita wore out the floorboards as she paced from room to room. Eventually, she retired to the bedroom.

"He says he's gonna handle things with Tony," Charles said as he got into bed.

"He did?" Rita asked. She was concerned Paul had brushed his father off, and Charles may not know the difference.

"That's what he told me," he said.

"Did he elaborate?" Rita couldn't believe this was all she was going to get.

"Do you really need me to answer that silly question?" Charles kissed her on the cheek. "You know how Paul can be." He snapped off the lamp on his nightstand and rolled over.

I sure do, Rita thought.

She was pleased to hear that things were better, but this report was hardly satisfying. A tangled web of frustration knotted in her chest. Rita missed her co-conspirator— Shannon was much better than Charles at sorting and dissecting the details.

DECEMBER 12TH

Paul

CHARLES ABERNATHY DIDN'T MAKE PHONE CALLS. IT wasn't his style. Paul knew his situation was starting to affect his parents when Dad called. And it was time to talk to Tony. What happened next was anyone's guess, but he couldn't be kept in the dark any longer.

One night after dinner, Paul locked himself in the garage and made the call. His boss answered on the second ring. Just as Paul was about to go into the script he'd been rehearsing for days, Tony invited him for a private catch-up at his home the next day.

Paul didn't sleep that night. He was so wracked with nerves he couldn't even bring himself to tell Shannon about the meeting. With his support system so tenuous, his anxiety was at an all-time high.

TONY OFFERED PAUL A CUP OF COFFEE AND THEN LED him to his home office where they could be alone. There were rows of framed photos of his ever-growing family on the credenza next to the large window behind his desk. Paul was touched to see his own family's photo alongside the Christmas cards that Shannon had mailed.

"I know it's been a while," Tony said. "I've been a bit distracted lately. Crazy time of year, huh?"

"Always is," Paul said.

"I wish some things in life could be easy, kid. You know my daughters don't want anything to do with this business. Never did. Years ago, one of Angela's boyfriends came to work for me. That lasted three days." Tony sneered at the memory.

Paul had questions. Lots of them. But he waited for Tony to say more.

"I remember when you first came knocking on my door for a job. I was in my prime back then. Top of my game. You learned from the best."

Tony's meaty laugh was tinged with nostalgia.

"Yes, I did."

Paul's eyes drifted out the window behind Tony. A few inches of snow had fallen overnight. The bare trees looked like skeletons staggered across the massive lawn.

"My sister's kid just graduated with a management degree," Tony said, sipping his coffee.

"He's taken over the storage room. Is he my new boss?"

Paul forced a nervous laugh that sounded as phony as it was.

"New boss? Of course not. I told my sister I would try and find a spot for him on my already sky-high payroll," Tony said. "After the divorce, the kid was spoiled. His old man would disappear for stints at a time. Those years were hell on my sister. Much as I'll always help family out, I can't hand my business over to a guy who doesn't know the difference between a hand auger and a jump rope."

This time Paul's laughter was real.

"What about Grayhall?" Paul asked.

"Grayhall?" Tony's furry black eyebrow raised to the ceiling as if controlled by a marionette.

"I saw his truck at the office a few Saturdays ago. I figured he was making an offer. Everyone knows Ralph's dying to buy you out. He has been for years."

"Yeah, but that doesn't mean I'd sell to *Grayhall*. What's gotten into you?"

"Why was he at the office?" Paul asked.

"I was working on the yearly bonuses. Ralph saw my van parked out front. He decided it was a good time to swing by and twist my onions. He picked up two Italian combos from Wawa, so we ate in my office. Can you imagine? Me and Grayhall breaking bread? I could hardly believe it myself! Anyway, I've been in and out of the office so much, I forgot all about it."

"So you're not looking to retire?" Paul asked.

"I didn't say that," Tony said. "I'm looking to get out by next spring, but I have a lot of loose ends to tie up before that happens."

Paul sipped his coffee and waited.

"You're the best employee I've ever had. Hard-working and loyal. I couldn't have asked for better. You need to know ... what I do is not a walk in the park," Tony said. "Running a business and managing a full staff is a lot of hard work. There will be a ton of headaches and more BS than you ever dreamed could land on your desk. You should know that first."

Paul leaned his head to the side. He wasn't following.

"I'll have my attorneys write up a promissory note. No money down. You'll pay me back over the next ten years. We'll make it a turnkey transfer of power."

Paul was stunned into silence.

"We don't get a lot of breaks in this life, but we get some. I wouldn't have all that I do if I hadn't gotten one or two along the way," Tony said. "Talk it over with Shannon and lawyer-up. I don't ever want you signing your name to anything without proper counsel. You hear me?"

"Yes, I do, boss!" Paul grinned and, for the first time in a long time, the knot in his stomach loosened. "I hear you," he repeated, "loud and clear."

Tony stood up from his desk and placed a heavy hand onto Paul's shoulder. His kind black eyes glistened like marbles. His bright white teeth popped against his smooth brown skin. Holding Paul's gaze was Tony's signature way of making sure his words had translated.

PAUL COULDN'T GET HOME FAST ENOUGH. THIS INcredible news would make things right between him and Shannon. She'd see he was still the same guy she had married, only better—not some angry dad who snapped at his kids over horseshit. Those days were over.

Paul stopped at the flower shop for a bouquet of white orchids on his way home.

When he arrived, Tamra was in the family room with the little girl from across the street. Miles' television blared from his bedroom, but Paul shook off the irritation. Tonight, nothing would bother him. He was going to be a business owner. Everything had changed. He had to get to Shannon.

P!nk serenaded Paul as he entered the kitchen. An open bottle of Prosecco chilled in the silver ice bucket they had received as a wedding present.

Shannon stood in front of the stovetop, lost in a daydream as she swayed and sang "A Million Dreams". The wooden spoon in her hand was new. That must have come from his mother. Shannon's utensils were plastic and bright in every shade of the rainbow. It was nice to see how the relationship between his mom and wife had blossomed. The image struck a shower of childhood memories. Home was his refuge after a long day at school. His mother's kitchen was his safe place to hide from the rest of the world. He became awash with a fresh wave of gratitude as he drank in the miracle of his loving wife.

"Oh!" Shannon said. "I didn't see you there."

"*P!nk* should have told you," Paul teased.

"What, honey?" She turned down the music.

Her face dropped when he handed her the orchids.

"Did Rita tell you already?" Shannon said.

"Tell me what, babe?"

"My good news."

"What's your good news?" Paul said.

"Something really great happened today."

Shannon filled two flutes with Prosecco and began her story.

Apparently, there were still cliques among grown women and a hierarchy. This particular tale centered around the pickleball clique at the gym.

"Well, Jenni, who's technically second-in-command of the pickleball clique, wanted to sign on. Then, when Brittany, the leader of the clique, saw what was going on, she swooped in to sign on. And then the most amazing thing happened!"

"What?" Paul tried to match her excitement.

"The three other women in the pickleball group signed up too! I have ten customers!"

"Wow!"

"This puts us in the black. My first paycheck will be added to our checking account the second week in January."

Paul hadn't seen her this lit from within in years. She was so animated and filled with happy tears, just like she had been on their wedding day. It was a sweet relief to have Shannon's blue-eyed shine back again.

The two worked in tandem, setting the table, fishing out the serving utensils, and dancing around the kitchen with prosecco. Shannon had prepared her roasted salmon covered in fresh pesto over couscous. It almost felt like they were on a trip somewhere and not stuck in their house in the middle of the holiday season with kids to feed. It would be time to call the kids for dinner soon.

"Honey," Shannon said. "What were the orchids for, if your mom didn't tell you my news?"

Paul felt like he was standing before two separate oceans as he peered into Shannon's eyes. He saw a little kid through the watery reflection. A kid who was still running from shadows, begging to be seen.

This is her moment.

"I don't need a reason to bring my incredible wife flowers," he said.

Shannon was giddy and made a silly face.

"Ten customers," he said. "I am so proud of you, baby."

He swept her into his arms with gentle strength as if he'd never let her go.

PART III

"You rose alone through winter's coldest storm,
But look how full you've grown."
~Angie Welland Crosby~

DECEMBER 12TH

Patti

THE RESPONSE FROM CHASE'S FOLLOWERS WAS BOTH wonderful and scary. To have customers dangling their credit cards became solid motivation, but Patti needed more staff and supplies.

As always, Rita was a big help and reached out to Paul for assistance. Being in the trades gave him access to locals thirsty for work.

Patti called two of the plumbers' wives who had been servers before they had kids. Dotti worked at *Harry's Ocean Bar and Grille*, and Barb worked at *The Rusty Nail*. They were able to commit to part-time positions. Both women reported to the bakery the next day for training.

Through all the commotion, Patti didn't have the time to process what was happening between her and Chase. Every day, he liaised with suppliers and ran outgoing orders to the post office. Christina trained the two new part-timers and covered the register. Patti kept the freezers stocked with dough, adding her finishing touches to outgoing orders. For the time being, the operation appeared to be working.

Then everything changed.

Patti was at the sink scrubbing a bowl and felt Chase come up behind her. She tapped the faucet off with her elbow, rubbed her hands on a dry towel, and turned around.

Chase shuffled on his feet. His neck and face were flushed. She hadn't seen him like this before. He was nervous.

"Do you have plans tomorrow night?" He spoke so quietly, she strained to hear him.

"Umm. I don't usually do anything. I mean, I don't usually go out. So, uh, no. I don't. I mean, I don't have plans," she stammered.

Patti wanted to disintegrate. She was so bad at this.

CHASE BROUGHT HER TO *EXIT ZERO FILLING STATION* on Sunset Boulevard in West Cape May. Instead of eating inside, Chase reserved the super cool silver Airstream trailer to enjoy their cozy meal in.

"I've been here a couple of times since being in town. The burgers are great," he said. "They have Cape May IPA, but tonight I may try the *Wicked Watermelon*."

Patti knew she had to taste the watermelon vodka drink infused with jalapeño simple syrup. They shared an order of Indian disco waffle fries to share served with pickled red onions, goat cheese, and red peppers in a cheesy-curry sauce. For entrees, Patti picked *A Christmas Curry* with chunks of chicken, roasted butternut squash, Brussels sprouts, carrots, peppers, and spiced pumpkin seeds in a green curry sauce. Chase ordered the *Thai Lobster* with mushrooms in a medley of spices and scooped a helping into a separate dish for her to try—it was a thrill for Patti to be out with a guy who approached mealtime as passionately as she did.

"My Aunt Mary would have adored this place. She taught me how to be a 'foodie' even before I knew what the word really meant."

"Sounds like you had a pretty good ally in your aunt," Chase said.

"I did. We had each other's backs. I still think about how mad Mom would get when she arrived," Patti said. "Aunt Mary was very particular about things. She'd rattle off a list of requests. Watching Mom squirm was hilarious."

"What was your favorite thing to make together?" Chase asked.

"Almond scones."

"Of course. I should have known. Yours are the best I've ever tasted. I'm not kidding," he said.

Patti knew he wasn't.

"Having my aunt there changed things for me," she said. "My mother was always wrapped up with her latest boyfriend, and my sister was obsessed with being skinny. I never really felt a part of anything until Aunt Mary showed up."

"She's a part of your life story forever," he said.

Patti knew it. She felt her aunt with her every day she sank her fingers into a fresh dough ball.

"It's weird how inspiration can smack you right in the face, but take years before you see the message," she said.

"Yeah, but you figured it out. You're living the dream. This is what you were made for. Do you know how important that is? People spend decades pondering and never figure out their purpose. It's everything."

Patti speared a disco fry with her fork. "Well, I do love food. I guess that's obvious." She slid the fry into her mouth.

"That's one of my favorite things about you," Chase said. "If you haven't noticed, I love good cuisine myself."

Patti had noticed his strong penchant for all things culinary, but he had height on his side and wore it well.

He moved his chair closer to hers.

"You know, of all the things I expected when I came back here, you weren't one of them," he said.

Her pulse quickened. She took a quick swallow of water to wash down the last bite of food.

"I like you a lot," he continued. "Rita was the only reason why I didn't say anything."

"You call your mother Rita now?" Patti smiled coyly.

"Only sometimes. When she's not around. Let's keep that between us, shall we?"

"I'll do my best not to let it slip out," she said.

He ran his fingers through his hair.

"I try not to make a habit of hitting on my mom's friends."

Patti's cheeks were sore from smiling, like they were on her graduation day.

Chase slid a bent finger down her cheek ever so tenderly and glanced at her slightly parted lips.

"I have something to tell you."

DECEMBER 14TH

Rita

RITA FELT LIKE AN INNKEEPER IN A CHRISTMAS MOVIE on the Hallmark channel. The enchantment of playing hostess to the folks passing through on the candlelight walking tours was like living in a fairy tale.

The visitors were polite and mostly quiet, yet much to her delight, there was always one or two in the group wanting to make small talk. They were filled with wonder and asked how the Abernathys came to be the current owners. She was sure to give proper reverence to the Bentley family and their impeccably high standards in maintaining the inherent beauty of the glorious landmark that was now Rita's home. As she spoke of stick work, cylindrical turrets, and pitched roofs, Rita heard Mr. Bentley's words poking through and took great pride in filling his shoes.

During their last phone call, Shannon mentioned she'd be coming into town for some last-minute Christmas shopping and to retrieve Tamra's lucky unicorn, which she had left behind during their visit.

Just as Rita expected, her daughter-in-law was floating from her shopping high. She sported a flamingo pink *Cape Mayniac* cap.

"Where did you get that?" Rita said. "I love it!"

"*West End Garage*," Shannon said. "There's an entire line of products, including mugs, magnets, T-shirts, and sweatshirts."

"How fun," Rita said. "Were you able to squeeze in a clam chowder soup from *The Ugly Mug* like I suggested?"

"Not yet, but I did grab a lobster roll from the *Cape May Fish Market*."

"Atta girl!"

Rita knew Shannon was going to love the restaurant scene in Cape May and was planning a Mother's Day brunch at *Oyster Bay Bar & Restaurant* for PEI mussels and St. Germain spritzes.

Shannon crowed over the goodies she picked up in town: three bottles of white balsamic vinegar from the *Cape May Olive Oil Company*, Jammin' Jamaican Java from *Love The Cook*, and a party box from the *Peanut Butter Co.*

"These make great teacher gifts. I'm also in three Secret Santa exchanges with the class moms, the pickleball club, and my business partners," she said.

Tamra was off exploring the house with her lucky unicorn in tow. The women made themselves comfortable in the parlor.

"Any word on our l-o-v-e birds?"

Shannon spelled out words she didn't want heard by Tamra, who had ears as large as the big bad wolf from *Little Red Riding Hood*.

"You-know-who has been pretty quiet on social media," Shannon added.

"Here's what I know: A few nights ago, they went on a second d-a-t-e," Rita said.

"This makes me so happy," Shannon said. "I can see why he likes Patti."

Rita felt the vibration of two little feet shuffle in from behind.

"Who likes Patti?" Tamra said.

Shannon looked at Rita, who grinned, pulling her granddaughter onto her lap.

"Come here, pretty girl. My oh my, you're getting so big now. Grammi can hardly lift you anymore."

"You're not the only one." Shannon sighed.

Just as Rita was about to ask if there were any new updates on Paul, Chase walked through the front door.

"Uncle Chase!" Tamra hopped off Rita's lap and attached herself to her uncle's waist.

"Whoa," he said. "This is a nice surprise."

"Our star of the show left her lucky charm here. Her play is Saturday night," Shannon said. "A girl needs her unicorn before she takes the stage."

"Uncle Chase, are you coming to see my play?" Tamra asked, still clinging to him.

"You bet. I wouldn't miss it." Chase patted her lightly on the back.

His eyes scanned the bags and packages splayed across the table from Shannon's shopping trip.

"Looks like Christmas came early," he said. "Hope I'm on Santa's good list this year."

"Mommy went shopping!" Tamra's exuberance made everything sound super fantastic.

Rita talked up Shannon's new business endeavors, knowing full well Chase would provide some much-needed enthusiasm.

"I didn't know anything about this. Good for you, sis." He nodded.

"You always put out such great content online," Shannon said. "You're so inspiring."

"I'll be more than happy to show you a few things. Anytime you want."

"I'm getting better at reels, but I need a stronger magnet. And I'm not sure how to set up a sales funnel," Shannon said.

"This all sounds very complicated," Rita said.

"Piece of cake." Chase winked.

"I have an idea. Dad and I planned on stopping at the house before the play on Saturday. Perhaps we'll come an hour or so early and you can show Shannon some things on the computer."

"That'd be great!" Shannon said.

Tamra was tuned in to her mother's moods and did a series of pirouettes.

"All good. I'll let our friends over at the bakery know I'll be punching out a little early this weekend." Chase winked again at the women.

Rita and Shannon exchanged side glances, as their lips twitched.

LATER THAT EVENING, RITA AND CHARLES ENJOYED A brandy by the fire. She took the opportunity to remind him what a great idea it was to buy their home and how lovely it was to see Shannon and Tamra enjoying the town. Living in Cape May was the gift that kept on giving, but she held back on mentioning the magic, if just this once.

"I'd like to hire a babysitter for Shannon. She needs more time to focus so she can get her work done. Tamra is going through a clingy stage," she said.

Charles raised the snifter to his lips as he took in this new information.

"Fine by me," he said, "but I doubt Paul will go for it."

"You don't think he'll let us do this for Shannon?" Rita asked.

"He's always been too proud for his own good," he said. *Sounds familiar*, Rita thought.

Unfortunately, Paul had picked up some of Charles' least favorable qualities. Paul could be obstinate to his own detriment. She wondered if anything could scale the walls he'd built around himself—or anyone.

DECEMBER 15TH

Patti

"BEING BACK IN CAPE MAY HAS CHANGED ME."

Chase's words had stunned Patti on their last date.

"I finally get why Mom wanted to buy this house. Some of our best memories as a family happened right here in this special place. All those summers and holidays. There are picture frames all over the house to prove it. Next time you're in the powder room on the first floor, check out the picture of Paul and me in front of *Hot Dog Tommy's*. Now *that* was a great summer! We got these long boogie boards in Avalon. I shredded mine before August that year from nailing the jetty. We drove my parents crazy, but it was a blast."

Chase squeezed his eyes closed and wiped his brow, as if drying out from the flood of memories.

"You know how I mentioned I was ready for a new chapter?" he said.

"Yes." Patti tried to conceal her building excitement.

"Well, I decided to take the show off the road for a while. I've been getting slammed with new clients for consultations and media training. I told you I think my mother's onto something with all that Cape May magic talk."

He wrapped his thick and strong arms around her waist like a harness.

"I mean, there's gotta be some magic here. I found you."

His words latched onto her heart like an old love song.

Patti didn't know where this was going or what came next. She only knew for as long as she lived, she'd never forget the way Chase kissed her that night.

THE BELLS JINGLED AS RITA ENTERED THE BAKERY.

"Good afternoon."

She wore a dress in Charles' family tartan and a pointy red knit hat with a pom-pom at the top. Even though Charles was born in Pennsylvania, his Scottish roots stretched for miles.

"You look adorable," Patti said.

"I told you to never call me that word." Rita snickered.

"It's good to see you in the Christmas spirit. When is Tamra going to be in *The Nutcracker*?"

"Tomorrow evening. Oh!" Rita pulled out her phone. "Wait till you see her costume. She is just delightful."

Rita scrolled through dozens of photos. Patti tried not to be obvious as she pored over the ones of Chase. He carried a quiet confidence with a tilted head and eyes that challenged the camera.

"I know you said you won't be seeing your sister this year. I hope you'll join us for Christmas," Rita said. "It'd be so lovely to have you there."

"I'd love to come. We close early on Christmas Eve. I'll bake some cinnamon twists with extra frosting on the side for the kids. I know they're both dunkers like their Uncle Chase."

Rita blushed. Patti felt like she had slipped. They hadn't yet spoken about her involvement with Chase.

Luckily, he walked in after dropping off the gifts for the foster kids, diffusing the awkward moment.

"Howdy," Chase said, sounding just like Charles.

"Hello, sweetheart," Rita said and turned to Patti. "How about some breakfast at our secret spot next week?"

"Sounds good to me," Patti said.

They watched Rita walk out. She looked like an actor on her way to the *Cape May Stage*, preparing for the next show.

"It's cute how shy your mom gets around us," Patti said. "Her visits were longer before you got to town."

"Hold up. You and my mom have a secret spot? I'm jealous," Chase said.

"We do. Sorry. I can't tell you where it is or it won't be a secret anymore," she said.

Chase grinned like they were sharing an inside joke.

"Please tell me you're coming for Christmas," he said.

"I'm coming for Christmas."

"That makes me so happy. I didn't know if you were going to see your sister."

"Not this year. They're taking the kids to Disney for Christmas week."

Chase waited for more.

"We're different people. She's obsessed with her fancy exercise bike, and I bake bread for a living."

"You mean a Peloton?" Chase said.

"What's that?" Patti asked.

"The fancy exercise bike."

"Is that what it's called? I'm not really the gym rat type."

She folded her arms across her abdomen.

Chase embraced her. "I like the type you are."

"Then I guess you landed in the right bakery."

Chase held her face with both hands and gave her a perfectly respectable kiss.

"I have to ask you something," he said.

Patti held still.

"What should I get Mom for Christmas?"

"Hmm. You can make her a nice finger painting for her fridge."

"There's an idea!"

"Moms like Rita are so simple. Just having you home is enough of a gift. She's been talking about this big family Christmas since they closed on the house last winter."

"Has she?" he asked.

"Yes. She also texted me pretty late the night you arrived," Patti said.

"I didn't realize how tight you and my mom are. That's really cool."

"I mean, we do have our own secret spot," she said.

"Well, if you guys are BFFs then you should know what she wants for Christmas."

"I do," she said.

Chase squeezed her arm and smiled dreamily.

"She wants you to make things right with your brother," Patti said gently.

His smile faded like a setting sun.

EGG HARBOR TOWNSHIP, NJ

ᴅECEMBER 16TH

THE NUTCRACKER AT STARDUST ELEMENTARY

Paul

OVER THE COURSE OF HIS LIFE, PAUL COULD REMEMBER specific instances where he felt both thrilled and terrified. Flying down the hill with no hands on his bicycle came to mind, as did the time Shannon's water broke when she was pregnant with Miles. As Tony showed him the ropes of running the company, Paul had those same feelings again.

He'd spent the week shadowing Tony's wife, Sheila, who carried a ton of responsibility. She filled in over the years as needed and knew most aspects of the business. Every day, she'd pick up the mail from the P.O. box and separate the bills from the checks. Then she'd stamp the checks, prepare the deposit slip, leave a copy on Tony's desk, and head to the bank. She also trained new office staff on the phones and clerical duties, managed the company's 401K plan, called in payroll, typed all company communications on letterhead, and could rattle off the price list by heart since she was the one who updated it every January.

Unfortunately, his boss wasn't the only one looking forward to retirement—Tony and Sheila were a package deal. Paul was not going to have the luxury of her taskmaster prowess, and he certainly couldn't pull Shannon in now. It became evident that he was going to need to learn how to run interviews.

He still hadn't told Shannon about Tony's offer. His plan was to surprise everyone with the news on Christmas Eve. She'd cry, of course. So would Mom, who was going to be especially proud after the advice she gave him. Dad would dole out quippy wisdom with an endearing cliché. Part of him wished his brother hadn't made it home for Christmas. He just wanted one night, one moment, where Chase didn't suck all the attention from the room.

On his drive home from work, Paul thought about the conversation he and Tony had earlier that day.

"So let me get this straight," Tony said. "First, you thought Ralph Grayhall, of all creeps, was buying me out? Then you thought that I was handing the golden key to Sheila's nephew who thinks a wrench is a prehistoric torture device?"

Paul laughed.

"You need to speak up. You're in charge now. If you have a question about something, ask it."

"Will do, boss."

Tony's parting words rattled around Paul's head for the remainder of the drive.

"Life will try to harden you. It's your job to not let that happen. You were guarded from the day we met. I figured you were just wet behind the ears and all. Being too hard-headed is not a sustainable way to go through life. Real men, strong men, show their vulnerability. Trust your instinct."

IT WAS OPENING NIGHT FOR *THE NUTCRACKER* AT Stardust Elementary. After seeing all the work Shannon put in, Paul understood why parents got so wrapped up in these types of productions. She'd spent weeks volunteering to help with costumes and running errands in between pick-ups and drop-offs. He couldn't believe the stuff she had managed to get done without complaint.

He stared out the window, awaiting his family's arrival.

"They should be here any minute," Shannon said.

She'd been looking forward to her computer lesson with Chase. Paul had mixed feelings about all that. He was careful not to say anything that would dampen his wife's joy, but he had a hard time shaking the feeling that his brother just wanted a piece of the spotlight.

He thought of Tony and wondered how he'd handle the situation. One thing he wouldn't do is lose his cool and over-react—Tony always kept his shit together.

His parents' SUV pulled into the driveway. He saw Chase at the wheel.

Trust your instinct.

Paul headed to the front door to greet his family.

DECEMBER 16TH

THE NUTCRACKER AT STARDUST ELEMENTARY

Rita

"Thank you so much for helping Shannon, sweetheart," Rita said.

Chase was chauffeuring her and Charles to see Tamra in *The Nutcracker*. They left early for Shannon's first computer lesson. He'd made a considerable impact on Patti's bottom line, and Rita was hopeful he'd do the same for Shannon.

"No need to thank me. She's my sister-in-law. I'd do anything for her."

Rita admired his great big heart which hadn't diminished a lick since boyhood.

"What did Patti have to say about you leaving work early today?" Rita asked.

"She went wild with jealousy," he teased. "You ever see a baker worked up? They can make a real mess. Flour is just as bad as glitter—it gets on everything. No, seriously, Patti's got plenty of coverage tonight. She's golden."

Rita opened her mouth to ask a question, but refrained midstream. She'd been good about not prying or getting involved and didn't want to blow that now.

"We're completely crazy about each other, by the way," Chase said. "You can stop wondering."

"Oh, honey! Really?" Rita was overjoyed.

"Really."

"That's good to hear, son," Charles said. "Patti's a real sweetheart."

Rita was dying for more, but they had just pulled into Paul's driveway.

She and Charles hadn't been there since Thanksgiving. The house now looked more like a holiday boutique. Motorized snowmen and women dressed in winter clothes held candles and sheets of music. The Christmas village that Rita and Charles had given them as newlyweds was set up on the window next to Shannon's homemade gingerbread house.

A noisy locomotive chugged around the room and circled the enormous Christmas tree that swallowed the modest living space with gobs of silver tinsel dripping from its branches. Decorating for the holidays was another passion the women shared.

SHANNON'S LAUGHTER COULD BE HEARD FROM THE den. Chase had a way of making everything interesting and fun.

"Grammi, my tummy hurts." Tamra bounced in her shiny silver shoes, rubbing her tiny belly with both palms.

"You just have a little performance anxiety, sweetheart," Rita said.

"What's that?"

"Come. Let's get you some crackers to nibble on."

She ushered her granddaughter into the kitchen.

Once they reached the hallway, her breath hitched.

Rita stood in disbelief as Chase and Paul disappeared into the garage.

DECEMBER 16TH

THE NUTCRACKER AT STARDUST ELEMENTARY

Paul

THEIR LITTLE CAPE WAS MORE ACTIVE THAN USUAL. His mother gushed over Tamra's hair and makeup in the bathroom. Miles cracked jokes with Grandpa in the family room. Shannon spoke excitedly on the phone in the den. Paul found himself awkwardly positioned next to his brother, standing halfway between the kitchen and hallway.

"Thanks for helping out with all that," Paul said, indicating to Shannon in the den.

"Sure thing."

Their father's laughter bellowed through the halls of the small house.

"Is there somewhere we can talk?" Chase asked.

"Uh, sure. Follow me."

Paul led him to the garage. It wasn't as cool as a man cave, but it was the only spot in the house that was his.

"What's up?" Paul asked.

"I've been all over this country. I forgot how special it is to be in Cape May during the holidays," Chase said.

"Yeah." Paul wondered where this conversation was going.

"Remember the time we scared the crap out of Mom on that dark street behind *The Southern Mansion*?" Chase asked.

It took a beat, but Paul's heart remembered.

"Corgie Street."

"Yes! Corgie Street. Mom was going through her ghost story phase at the library and kept creeping herself out. I thought she was gonna kill you when you jumped out at her," Chase said.

"What? I didn't jump out at her," Paul said. "You pushed me and started rattling the gate, making all those weird sounds."

Chase thought on this. "You may have a point."

"Jerk." One corner of Paul's mouth lifted.

"Either way, it's good to be back here. I got something I want to run by you."

Paul's head spun as he listened to his brother's plans. He was setting up a small business. The traveling was getting to him. The key piece of information was that Chase was not leaving—he was staying in Cape May.

"That's cool." Paul didn't know what else to say.

"I wanted to tell you before Mom and Dad," Chase said. "I know things are a little awkward. I just don't want to get in the way."

"You're never around long enough to get in the way," Paul said.

Hurt spread across his brother's face.

"The last time you came to visit, it felt like you were just using us as a pit stop."

Paul surprised himself, but there it was in all its glory—the naked truth. Tony would be proud.

"A pit stop? No way, man. Never!" Chase shook his head.

"I'm just telling you how it seemed," Paul said.

"I came because I wanted to see you, Shannon, and the kids." Chase's eyes were dewy which spoke of his sincerity. "We lead our own lives. It's not as uncommon as you think. Patti and her sister are nothing alike," Chase added.

Paul hadn't known how serious his brother was about Patti until that moment—it softened him.

"You're that guy with the whole life package: the drop-dead gorgeous wife and two great kids," Chase said. "You're the diligent one. I didn't have your focus."

"You mean intensity?" Paul raised the same corner of this mouth again.

"That either. You're the family guy with the steady job. I like to explore."

"And now?"

"I don't really have a place to call home. It's probably time to change that." Chase rubbed his palms together.

Trust your instinct. Tony's words still lingered.

"I have something to tell you, too," Paul said.

It was in that moment Paul knew he wanted Chase to be the first to know. Their father tried to get it out of him on their last phone call, but that wasn't how Paul wanted to break the surprise, and there was no way Dad would have been able to keep it from Mom. She had ways of figuring things out just like Shannon. And he knew the women were talking up a storm behind his back.

This news was life-changing for him. It validated him. All those years slogging through work every day had not been in vain.

"Are you telling me that Tony is selling you the business?" Chase asked.

"I'll be paying him back over the next ten years," Paul said. "But yeah."

"Congratulations, man!" Chase slapped him on the back, which felt more rewarding than a hug. "That's huge."

Paul put his hands in his pockets and looked down. A prideful smile bloomed on his face.

"Mom's gonna blast this news all over. She'll probably reserve one of those airplane banners to fly over the beach next summer," Chase said. "Sunbathers need to keep well-informed, ya know."

Paul laughed. "I could totally see her doing that."

"Shannon must be happy."

"She doesn't know yet," Paul said.

Chase's lips parted, his eyebrows lifted.

"I almost told her the day it happened, but it wasn't the time," Paul said.

"Who else knows?" Chase asked.

"No one," Paul said. "Just you. I figured I'd wait and surprise everyone on Christmas Eve."

"I tell you there's gotta be something to that Cape May magic Mom keeps going on about."

"Don't bring that up in front of Dad," Paul said.

"I know he's tired of hearing it, but I think she's right."

Paul glanced at his watch. "We better get going. It's almost showtime for my little girl." He headed for the door leading back to the house.

"Hang on a second, bro."

Paul stopped walking and turned around.

"Thank you for trusting me with this awesome news. I'm really proud of you." Chase held a fist to his chest and nodded in reverence.

If Paul could articulate the words in his heart, he'd thank his brother for making him feel so good. He'd tell him how glad he was that he came home for Christmas and that he missed having a brother. He'd admit how much he loved Chase and remind him that he always would.

Instead, Paul followed his big brother's lead.

He nodded, tucked his bottom lip, and pressed a solid fist against his pounding heart.

PART IV

The future lies before you, like a field of fallen snow;
Be careful how you tread it, for every step will show."
~Doris A. Wright~

DECEMBER 21ST

Patti

ON THE NIGHT OF THE WINTER SOLSTICE, CHRISTINA got her Christmas wish for a double date with Patti and Chase. They stopped in at her and Derek's for appetizers and cocktails. She prepared a traditional Puerto Rican Christmas spread, including the Diaz family's beloved coquito. Patti was introduced to the creamy, tropical eggnog in culinary school, made with cream of coconut, spices, and rum.

Naturally, Chase enjoyed the festive beverage as much as Patti did.

"This is the best coquito I've ever had," he said, swiping a napkin across his mouth.

Chase was already a smash hit with Christina, and now he was warming to Derek.

Patti enjoyed being with him in the company of others. When they were alone, their conversations had a more intimate feel, based around their goals and dreams. With Christina and Derek, Chase spoke of his travels and the compulsion he had to showcase and honor small-town living. Patti could see from their faces she was not the only one who had been taken by Chase's ability to turn the ordinary into the exceptional.

As the night wore on, Christina pulled Patti into the kitchen and left the guys in the living room.

"Looks like I was right about you two," Christina said.

"Well, you were the one shoving his website in my face!"

"Shhhh." Christina dropped her voice. "I'm so glad that you finally listened to me. I told you he liked you."

"Yes, you did. I couldn't see it. Guys like Chase don't usually go for girls like me. He's *way* too hot," Patti said.

"No, he's not. I mean, yes, he's hot, but so are you, amiga. He's the luckiest dude in Cape May," Christina said. "Well, not including Derek, of course."

"But of course." Patti loved the kick she got out of her lovestruck friend.

THEIR NIGHT WAS WINDING DOWN; CHASE AND DEREK pulled each other into that half-hug that guys sometimes do.

"Are you sure it's okay if I share the recipe on my site? I promise to give your family full credit," Chase said to Christina.

"More than okay." She kissed him on the cheek.

"We definitely need to hang again, man," Derek said.

"For sure. If you guys want to meet up next Wednesday night, I know my girl loves to hear *The Squares* perform over at *The Mad Matter*," Chase said.

"Let's do it!" Christina said.

"Sound good to you, Patti-cake?" Chase asked.

Patti's cheeks warmed as he smiled adoringly at her. It was the first time Chase referred to her as his girl, and the nickname was new. She was only too glad Christina got to hear it.

The guys continued to blather on.

"*Patti-cake*? The guy is smitten. Derek said he's been talking about you all night," Christina whispered to Patti.

Chase made her feel like she was on top of the world—as if owning a bakery in a beach town was the pinnacle of success. The way he lauded her all night to Derek only validated her path. She was pretty darn sure Aunt Mary would approve of her choice and then some.

"It's la magia," Christina said.

Patti needed to brush up on the Spanish she learned in high school.

"I don't remember that word."

"It means *the magic*," Christina said. "What your man's mother always talks about."

"Rita told you about the Cape May magic too?" Patti was incredulous.

"Sí, and she knows what she's talking about. Just look around us. We got two good ones."

Patti looked over at the guys who were still yucking it up.

"We sure do, my friend," she said.

Christmas Eve

Patti tried on four different ensembles with three pairs of shoes. Her black pants were snugger than the last time she tried them on, but it was the holiday season; it was only natural for the local baker to be stuffed like a Christmas goose. Patti snort-laughed to herself. Anything would be a welcome change from the Frosty-the-Snowman look she wore every day in her chef whites. She slipped on her cherry-red sweater and black snow boots. The multi-colored gemstones of Aunt Mary's Christmas tree brooch reflected in the mirror.

At the start of the season, Patti stood helpless in the face of supply chain issues, packed crowds, and long hours. And while she still had those same concerns, somehow everything turned around. The helplessness was gone. With Chase's cool intellect and contagious energy by her side, no problem seemed insurmountable.

Patti had been looking forward to spending Christmas with the Abernathys and hoped for more time to get to know Shannon. She'd heard from both Rita and Chase about how hard she'd been working on her skincare line. It wasn't easy to get a business going, especially with two kids to handle. Patti didn't have a lot of extra money, but she made it a goal for the new year to become one of Shannon's clients.

There was a series of soft knocks on the front door. Chase had arrived. He had his own distinct pattern: *knock ... knock ... knock ... knock-knock-knock.*

He wore strands of holiday lights arounds his neck. Patti had to laugh.

"This is what you get when a six-year-old runs your life," he said. "Tamra didn't want you to feel foolish walking down the street without these, so here you go." He looped three sets of blinking lights around her neck.

"People are going to think we're nuts," she said.

"In Cape May? Nah. We look festive. Everyone will want a set of these babies."

He brandished a small white box from his coat pocket. The sticker on the front read *Janet Payne Jewelry*. Inside were handcrafted silver earrings made with stacked sea glass and freshwater pearls.

"These are beautiful!" Patti kissed him. "Thank you so much."

She slipped off her old silver hoops. The green-blue sea glass caught the light.

"The color matches your pretty eyes," Chase said.

Patti spotted a little note tucked inside the packaging that filled her with warmth.

*Some of the greatest treasures on the beach are not
the ones that fill your pockets; they are the ones that
fill your soul. –Janet Payne*

Chase was a ball of energy and more than ready to kick off the Christmas Eve festivities. Meanwhile, the silly necklaces made Patti feel like a blinking traffic light on Beach Avenue in the off-season.

"You're not gonna believe this," he said. "And I have you to thank."

"Me?"

Chase wrapped an arm around her as they walked. Patti nestled up against him, maintaining her stride. His enthusiasm was contagious.

"I talked to my brother. Just like you told me to."

"That's great."

"And that's not all," he said with a toothy grin.

As he spoke, Patti thought back to the first time she met Rita. Her desire to get things just right for the family's first Cape May Christmas was palpable. Namely, she wanted her sons to be close again. After hearing from Christina, it was clear to see how powerful Rita's belief was. It warmed Patti to know her friend's wish had come true. Maybe Chase was right; maybe Rita was onto something.

The more Patti thought about it, the more she started to see and feel the magic all around them—either that or it was the flashing disco lights hanging from their necks.

CHRISTMAS EVE

Rita

IN HER FORTY YEARS WITH CHARLES, RITA'S CHRISTMAS Eve table had never looked like a spread in *Town & Country*—until then. The cloth covered the large pine table, matching the twelve high-back chairs upholstered in a burgundy damask. Decorative bowls filled with Poinsettias adorned the gold-leaf table runner. Ivory tapered candles surrounded with boughs of holly flickered in greeting as each guest entered the dining room. In front of each place setting, ceramic angels in white gowns that matched the angel at the top of her Christmas tree held name cards for each guest. The cream-colored silk napkins were tied with twine and a sprig of evergreen. She had turned on the light display for her snow globe collection, which provided the perfectly elegant backdrop to the winter scape.

"What a feast!" Patti said. "Does she always go all out like this?"

Shannon nodded. "Rita's half Italian. Christmas Eve was a pretty big deal on her mom's side of the family."

"My mother was the baby of eight. I had twenty-two first cousins on the Del Vecchio side, if you can believe that," Rita said.

"I can't believe Nonna had seven brothers and sisters. No wonder she was a little nutty," Paul said.

"More than a little," Charles chimed in.

"Hey, now. It's Christmas Eve. No picking on Nonna. She's not here to chase us with a wooden spoon, yelling slurs in her native tongue," Rita joked.

Charles bellowed.

"I can't believe I didn't know any of this about you," Patti said.

"You mean Mom forgot to mention crazy Nonna when you were in your secret spot together?" Chase quipped.

"What's that?" Shannon crinkled her nose.

"Patti and I have a clandestine meeting spot for breakfast. Next time you'll join us," Rita said, "but you must keep it a secret. No boys allowed."

"Do you hear this?" Chase elbowed Paul. "Mom's finally got the two daughters she always wanted, and we've just been downgraded to second-class citizens."

"Tell me about it." Paul sighed. "Thanks a lot, *Grammi*."

"Starting to feel like chopped liver over here." Chase exaggerated a frown.

Rita was overjoyed to see the boys teaming up—even if it was at her expense.

"And they say girls are melodramatic? Puh-lease ..." she said.

Even the grandchildren laughed.

Rita's Christmas Eve spread took days to prepare but was well worth the effort. She'd created a printed menu card for each guest. Patti was near-drooling as Shannon and Chase brought large platters of food to the table. Miles filled the salad bowls. Paul sliced pepperoni and chunks of gouda for the charcuterie board. Charles and Patti made light conversation over glasses of Chianti.

Rita Abernathy's Christmas Eve Menu 2023

~Starters~

Crudités

Charcuterie board

Little necks

Bruschetta with lump crab

~Sides~

Garlic bread

Chickpea salad

Broccolini in garlic and olive oil

~Entrees~

Zuppa di pesce fra diavolo over capellini

Shrimp parmigiana

Eggplant lasagna

~Dolce~

Gingerbread cookies

REINDEER PRETZEL BITES

TIRAMISU

STRUFFOLI

*CROISSANT ASSORTMENT AND CINNAMON TWISTS WITH
VANILLA FROSTING, COURTESY OF *PATTI'S PANTRY*.

*ALL SEAFOOD FROM *THE LOBSTER HOUSE FISH MARKET*.

For the next twenty minutes, the predominant sound in the room was stainless steel on china, interspersed with a few satisfied moans of delight. Rita watched her guests help themselves to seconds and thirds, as the wine carafes were emptied.

Miles filled his mother's glass with the last of the lemon water.

"Should I get more?" he asked, holding up the empty pitcher.

"Yes, please," Shannon said. "Thank you, sweetie."

They watched him leave the room.

"He's been awfully helpful this evening," Rita said.

"Yes, he has," Charles added. "He stacked all the firewood for me. You got a good boy there."

"We had a little talk with him," Shannon said.

"Let's hope it lasts through January," Paul said.

THE LAST FORKFUL OF PASTA AND SEAFOOD HAD BEEN swallowed. The dinner plates were cleared to make way for dessert. Charles set the percolator on the buffet with hot water for tea and after-dinner cordials. Their beautiful Christmas Eve dinner was coming to an end.

Unbeknownst to Rita, the night was just getting started.

Paul stood up from his seat and walked to the front of the room next to his father.

"I've got something to tell everyone." His voice faltered. Rita had no idea what he was about to say, but his nerves were in a bundle.

"Tony's retiring next spring," he said.

"What?" Shannon said. "Are you sure? When did you find this out?"

"We met a couple of weeks ago at his house. He wanted to talk."

Shannon squinted her eyes into half-moons. Apparently, Rita wasn't the only one who thought it was strange that Paul hadn't mentioned this.

He went on to explain the arrangement Tony offered with the promissory for the next ten years and spoke a bit about his plans and how much work there was ahead.

"I wanted to save the news and surprise you all for Christmas. So ... surprise!" he said.

"Oh, babe." Shannon jumped up. "I'm so happy!" She fell into Paul's arms.

"Fine job, son," Charles said. "Sounds like a grand slam to me."

"It sure is!" Rita was too stunned to add more. This news was better than anything she could have possibly concluded.

Suddenly, Chase joined his brother at the front of the room. Rita looked from one to the other. *What were these two up to?*

"My freelance work has exploded. I'll be grounded here for a while. Looks like Uncle Chase will be sticking around."

"Yay! Uncle Chase is staying!" Tamra bounced in her chair.

"Awesome!" Miles pumped his fist.

Paul raised his glass in his brother's direction.

"This guy's gonna help me leverage the internet to promote business. Time to bring this plumbing company into the twenty-first century."

"Looking forward to it, man," Chase said.

The sound of her sons' glasses joining in toast was nearly as precious as the Baby Jesus swaddled in their family creche.

Now Rita knew what they were discussing the day she saw them go into Paul's garage. Chase had been so cagey on the ride home after the play.

These were the Abernathy brothers she remembered. The ones who schemed and helped each other out. No matter how time affected the terrain of their lives, the landscape of their hearts remained intact.

Rita stood to congratulate her sons. She wrapped her arms around Paul first. Suddenly, she felt like they'd been caught in a human vice with another pair of arms.

"It's a Grammi sandwich!"

Chase enveloped Rita and Paul in his massive arm span, squeezing them tight.

"Hmm. This sandwich needs something. It's too dry," Chase said. "Where are my condiments? We need mustard and pickles to complete this Grammi sandwich, you guys."

Miles and Tamra followed their uncle's cue and raced to get in on the group hug. Rita became trapped at the epicenter of this massive pile-on made up of arms, hands, and bodies.

"Ahem, ladies? What about my lettuce and tomato?" Chase asked.

Shannon and Patti joined in on the fun.

"Oh, for heaven's sake," Rita said, but of course no one could hear her through all the giggling and shuffling about.

"Everybody say cheese!" Charles' voice boomed. How typical for him to be snapping photographs instead of saving his poor wife from being smothered—she'd get him later for this!

THE LAST DISHWASHING CYCLE OF THE EVENING AWAIT-ed. Rita stood at the sink with a wad of tissues pressed against her mouth. It had been ages since she cried so unabashedly from sheer joy.

"What a night, huh?" Shannon joined her at the sink.

"You're a damn good mother, Shannon. They don't come better. You're the daughter I always hope for."

It was Shannon's turn to get teary. Rita didn't want to miss the opportunity to let her daughter-in-law know how much she appreciated her. The season had been so much more enjoyable with all their many chats and laughs. She could hardly wait for Shannon to open the gigantic box of books wrapped under the tree.

"You're the best wing woman," Shannon said. "We're a great team."

"That we are." Rita dabbed the corner of her eyes. "It's a relief to see the guys together again. They were always keeping secrets. They even seemed to have their own language. There were times Charles and I couldn't understand a blessed word from their mouths. Such rascals they were."

"I've seen them communicate. It's strange and wonderful. Even the kids can't figure out what they're saying," Shannon said.

"I'm one proud momma to be sure."

"All right, what's going on in here?" Paul asked. "Geez, you two look like someone ran off with your lattes. It's Christmas. Time to get jolly!"

His levity was exactly what both women needed.

Rita eyed the microwave clock. "It's about that time."

"I'll wash up and gather the kids." Shannon went back to the dining room.

Rita looked at her son. A business owner. She could hardly believe how far Paul had come.

"You ready?" she said.

"More ready than you'll ever know," he replied.

"I'm very proud of you, sweetheart."

"I know you are, Mom. Thanks for saying it."

ON CHRISTMAS EVE, THE ABERNATHY FAMILY HAD A long-standing tradition of gathering around the tree before bed. The kids would cuddle under blankets in pajamas and nibble on Grammi's gingerbread cookies. Sometimes they'd take turns sharing excerpts from their favorite books or Christmas classics or simply read a poem. It was a collective and meaningful pause for their family, with no televisions or electronics.

Rita entered the living room just in time to catch Chase and Patti in a cozy moment. They were cuddled up on the loveseat next to the fireplace. Their shared smiles were as bright as a midnight star. They really made such a nice pair.

Tamra decided it was a good time to fawn over Patti the way little girls do when there's a big girl around. She examined the ocean-blue sea glass stack of the earrings Chase bought her—Rita was glad she had sent him to *Splash* to pick out something special.

"You're so pretty. I like your hair. I like your makeup. Your cheeks sparkle like glitter!"

The spirited six-year-old traced Patti's face with her grubby fingertips.

"Baby, it's impolite to touch people's faces. Let's give Patti some space, please." Shannon stifled a laugh as she pulled her from Patti's lap. Paul called Tamra over who marched across the room and plopped onto his lap, just as Miles returned from the bathroom.

"Where's Grandpa?"

Rita's eyes went to Charles' empty recliner. She hadn't noticed him leave.

"Grandpa, are you playing hide and seek?" Tamra asked.

"I'll go get him," Chase said.

"I'll go," Paul said.

"Everyone stay put. I'll be right back," Rita said.

She turned the corner and found Charles standing in the hallway.

"Good evening," he said. There was a book tucked beneath one arm and a tall glass of water in his hand.

"Everything all right?"

"Follow me." Charles led her back to the family room.

"Here's the big guy," Paul said.

"Here I am," Charles said. "My sources up at the North Pole tell me there was a messenger sent to this location earlier today."

Shannon whispered in Tamra's ear, who then scurried out of the room and returned a few beats later with a gift box.

"Here, Grammi!" She placed the box in front of Rita, stroking the ribbons like doll hair.

"Oh, my. What is this?"

"Here we go again," Paul said, half-smiling.

"Not this routine." Chase turned to Patti. "Mom likes to feign shock over every present she receives."

Paul busted out laughing.

"Hey, lady, heads up. It's Christmastime. There'll be more presents tomorrow." Paul pressed a hand to his chest, miming a look of horror.

"You two, hush up. What do we have here?" She opened the card and read in silence.

To my darling Rita,
May we never forget the first one.
Merry Christmas,
–Charles

Inside was a ten-inch snow globe with the words *The Abernathy Family Christmas Cape May, NJ 2023* engraved on the front. It had a key at the back to wind for music.

"Turn it over," Shannon said softly.

Rita steadied the heavy globe for a peek at the bottom. All of their names were carved into the wood—including Patti's.

"Chase thought it would be cool to remember everyone who celebrated the first Cape May Christmas," Paul said.

Rita ran her finger against the markings. Each and every one of these names would be engraved on her soul till the end of time.

Charles blew her a kiss and raised the book he had tucked beneath his arm.

"I thought this would be a good pick for Tamra who dazzled with her performance in *The Nutcracker*, making us all so proud."

Tamra swung her legs back and forth.

"This edition is one of the earliest known English translations of E.T.A. Hoffmann's classic children's tale, called *Nutcracker and Mouse-King*, which was penned in German in 1816." Charles cleared his throat and continued. "This translation by Mrs. St. Simon was making the story popular in the English-speaking world. The stage was set for Tchaikovsky to bring the story into the 20th century in his famous ballet. For centuries, this tale has delighted countless children and adults alike."

Charles took his seat. He crossed one leg over the other. All movement in the room ceased. The fire crackled as he turned to the first page.

"During the long, long day of the twenty-fourth of December ..."

CHRISTMAS EVE

Paul

PAUL FINALLY UNDERSTOOD THE DEEPER REASON HIS mother wanted to move to their favorite vacation destination. Being back together as a family brought a wave of good memories from that time in their lives.

Mom went out of her way to make things extra special, and that generosity was extended to both of his kids. Paul also knew his parents wanted to provide a free beach vacation for his family since money had been so tight. The more life he lived, the more he came to appreciate the sacrifices his parents always made on his behalf.

"Knock, knock." Paul lightly rapped the back of his knuckles on Miles' partially opened bedroom door.

Miles looked up.

"Hey, bud. Is it okay if I come in?" he asked.

Miles sat up. "Sure."

"You did good today. Thanks for helping Grammi and Grandpa out. It means a lot to me and Mom."

"I like helping them," Miles said.

He really was a good kid.

"I'm proud of you." Paul spit the words out before they got stuck. "I don't tell you as much as I should."

He leaned over and kissed his son.

"We better say goodnight now. We don't want Santa to skip over our house."

"Yeah, right ..." Miles said.

Paul winked and headed for the door. He didn't want to break down in front of his boy, who he wished was still young enough to believe in Santa Claus—those years went by too fast.

He saw traces of himself in Miles. It was hard being eleven and living in a perpetual state of confusion and frustration—when you're too old for the baby stuff, but too young to be taken seriously.

Paul had so many dreams for him and his family. Now that he was taking over the business and with the expansion of Shannon's operation, there was a little more wiggle room in the budget.

He found Shannon in their bedroom tying ribbons to last-minute stocking stuffers. She looked serene. On their wedding day, his father told him he was one lucky son of a gun. It wasn't just her outward beauty that made her so endearing; she had a childlike sweetness Paul hadn't noticed until after the kids were born.

He handed her a wrapped present.

"What's this?" Shannon asked.

"It's a Christmas gift, babe. Are you turning into my mother?"

Shannon chuckled and removed a folder from a wrapped package.

"You remember the rich architect I did that huge job for in Stone Harbor?"

"Yes." Shannon flipped through the pages inside.

"Well, she's helping me with a project."

Paul was adding an extension onto the back of their house. The plans included an office space for Shannon with enough room for a table and seating for guests.

"I don't know what to say." She looked up. "You're the best husband in the world!"

Paul had to laugh in spite of himself. How did a wretch like him end up with the dearest woman on the planet? Shannon was his rock. His anchor. He'd be lost at sea without her. They both knew it.

"You deserve it all, baby. I don't have the patience to handle one-third of the stuff you do. Come here." He pulled her in close. "You're my everything. Don't ever forget it. Okay?"

"Okay ..." Tears glistened the seashell-pink skin of her delicate face.

There were footsteps in the hallway. Rita poked her head in.

"Patti's getting ready to say goodnight."

They followed her downstairs.

When Paul reached the foyer, Patti looked up from buttoning her coat.

"Congratulations again," she said. "That's super great news about your new business."

"Thanks, Patti. It was real good having you with us tonight. You make this guy more bearable to be around."

Paul cocked his head toward Chase who smiled good-naturedly. His brother had always been a good sport about things—Paul had always admired that about him.

"Those cinnamon twists are out of this world. You're so talented," Shannon said.

"I can show you how to make them," Patti offered.

"Rita is *so* lucky to live right around the corner from a pastry chef," Shannon added.

"Let's just say my girdle is getting a lot of mileage this season. And I have Miss Kelley to thank for that." Rita squeezed Patti's arm. "The diet starts January."

"Now you're in the penalty box. You know the rules: no talk of dieting or counting calories on Christmas," Patti said.

"I like your style." Paul nodded.

"Well, goodnight, my kiddos." Rita headed for the stairs. "I love you all. Merry Christmas."

Paul, Shannon, Chase, and Patti echoed back in unison. "Merry Christmas!"

"Have you guys been to the steakhouse on Beach yet? It's called *Primal*. The five-star reviews have been pouring in," Patti said.

"The four of us should check that out some time," Chase said.

"I'd love to!" Shannon said.

"Let's do it," Paul said.

"Rita's been hitting me up for restaurant suggestions. She's compiling a list for you all for the spring and summer."

"Can we get a sneak peek?" Shannon asked.

"You definitely want to check out *The Cricket Club* on Decatur. That's the former Merion Inn."

"Which place has the *Bayou Oyster Stew* you were telling me about?" Chase asked.

"That's *410 Bank Street,*" Patti said. "They'll reopen in April."

"Okay, I'm getting hungry again," Shannon said. "How is that even possible?"

"My girl has a sophisticated palate." Chase beamed with pride. He hooked an arm around Patti and kissed her cheek.

"Mommy?" Tamra stood at the top of the stairs in a red velvet nightgown, clutching her lucky unicorn.

"Aren't you supposed to be asleep, Madame?" Shannon asked.

"Santa Claus better not see you out of bed," Paul said.

"Is Patti coming back tomorrow?" Tamra asked.

Shannon shrugged affably at Patti.

"Yes, I am. And I have a special surprise for you and Miles," Patti said sweetly.

Tamra's mouth flew opened and she bounced in place. It was a lot of excitement for a six-year-old to handle.

Paul could see his wife and kids were as taken with Patti as they were with Chase. The two made a perfect match. It was cool observing his brother through this new lens. He was solicitous with Patti, taking great care to be sure she was comfortable and at ease.

It struck Paul that Chase had ended up just like him and Dad.

They were three Abernathy men pummeled by love's tide.

As the winter solstice approaches, the chill in the air deepens, and the frosty grip of winter begins to tighten. Days grow ever shorter, and the nights are at their longest and darkest. It is, therefore, no wonder that December's full moon is known as both the Cold Moon and the Long Night Moon.

DECEMBER 27TH

Patti

PATTI AND RITA MADE SMALL TALK IN THE DINING room while Charles thumbed through the holiday issue of the *Cape May Magazine*. After two months of cooking and entertaining, Rita needed a break from all culinary duties, and Chase was preparing dinner for the four of them.

"Relax," he told his mom. "Sit."

"You sure we can't assist?" Rita called out.

"We're here to help," Patti added.

Chase emerged from the kitchen, wearing his *Patti's Pantry* apron. He dramatically slapped a rolled dishtowel over his shoulder like a short order cook.

"You two are worse than the kids. Didn't you ever learn that patience is a virtue?"

As Chase returned to the kitchen, the sumptuous aroma of garlic and onions wafted in their direction as the door closed behind him. Patti salivated.

"It's a good thing we had those gingerbread cookies earlier or we'd be gnawing our hands off." Rita pretended to nibble her fingertips.

"I'm about ready to start plucking gumdrops off that gingerbread house," Charles said.

The women erupted into laughter.

"Knock it off in there or you'll be sent to bed with no dinner," Chase called from the kitchen.

"I don't know where he gets this stuff from. I never sent either one of my boys to bed without supper." Rita shook her head.

"This is Chase we're talking about. I fact-check what he says before reacting," Patti said.

"You gals today are much sharper than I ever was," Rita said.

"Pardon me, ladies." Charles stood up and stretched his arms. "I'm going to wash up for dinner ... and maybe swallow some toothpaste to hold me over."

Rita smiled at Patti as Charles left the room.

"I love your family," Patti said sweetly. "Thanks so much for having me for Christmas."

"You're a part of our family. It wouldn't have been the same without you, darling." Rita patted her hand. "We'll always have a special connection thanks to your mother and my sister. Nothing will change that, my dear."

She slid a large packet with a gold bow across the table toward Patti.

"What's this? We already exchanged presents."

"It's just a little something extra. You have given me more than you could possibly imagine just by being in my life. Open it!"

Rita had signed Patti up to be Shannon's newest skin-care client.

"I was planning on saving to sign up for this."

"I'm a mother. We know stuff. I gotta take care of my two girls."

Rita brushed Patti's bangs out of her eyes and kissed her forehead. The gesture felt so exquisitely comforting that it pulled her back to her early childhood. Unbidden tears stung Patti's eyes. Rita pulled two tissues from the box and handed her one.

"Look at us. Just a couple of saps." Rita dabbed her eyes. "It's good to cry. Crying heals us."

Crying heals us.

Patti would hold on to this keepsake from her treasured friend.

BACK AT PATTI'S APARTMENT, SHE AND CHASE SAT ON her sofa looking through the front window at the full moon.

Her entire life had shifted over the last month, yet from the outside nothing seemed all that different. Chase made her look at things in new and exciting ways. Thanks to him, she added a tagline to her brand.

Patti's Pantry: The Taste of Coming Home.

"Your parents are special," she told him. "You're lucky."

"They are. And they love you. I hope you know that."

Patti was comforted by his words. Rita and Charles were so dear to her.

"I have a secret to share," he said.

She could feel the strength of his sinewy arm flexing through his flannel shirt as her back pressed into the couch.

"They're not the only ones," he said softly.

Patti once heard the moon reflects in all directions when struck by the sun. That was how she felt when Chase came into her life. He showed her the limitless possibilities swirling all around them like flurries in a snow globe.

Rita

THE FRENETIC ENERGY OF THE HOLIDAY SEASON SUR-
rendered to the languorous pace of winter in the week between Christmas and New Year's. The suspension in time
ushered in forgotten memories of holidays long ago. Rita
grew mesmerized by the raging snowstorm taking place inside her newest snow globe. She wound the key at the back.
"It Came Upon the Midnight Clear" filled the empty room
like a lullaby.

A vision of a young mother came into focus. She was
standing by her kitchen window, stirring a batch of soup
and watching her children frolic and play across a snowy
landscape. She set out some dry clothing and filled their
soup bowls, preparing to call them in from the frigid temps.
The grandfather clock struck midnight, snapping Rita back
to the present. Time whispered its fleeting essence with every swing of the pendulum.

The fire dwindled. A tired but comforting sense of calm
settled into her bones. Rita couldn't remember the last time
she'd felt such serenity, such contentment. Certainly not

since becoming a mother—maybe as a new bride. That was an exciting time. All those possibilities and years still ahead of them. *Where would they live? How many children would they have? Would the kids take after her or Charles?*

How does one reconcile those early days of wonder with a life that's already been lived? She was still that same bashful bookworm, now living out a real-life fairy tale in her own Victorian home. Her fingers brushed the bottom of the snow globe, tracing each name. Their first Cape May Christmas was a smashing success. She and Charles couldn't have found better companions for their sons if they had discovered Shannon and Patti from a Christmas catalog.

She set the snow globe on the front picture window amidst the Christmas village and sipped a mug of spiced mulled wine to keep warm. Charles moved in behind her. He netted her shoulders with his large, gentle hands. His enviable height allowed him to rest his chin on the top of her head.

"There you are," he said. "Did you get a load of that moon earlier?"

"For a minute I thought someone turned on the flood lights," Rita said.

They stood, as one, looking out the front window. There was a young couple huddled together on the sidewalk. They were taking photos of the Abernathy's home. Rita was flooded with pride and gratitude to be living inside a Cape May gem with the lit Christmas tree and fireplace at their backs.

Rita raised her palm. The couple waved back.

"Do we know them?" Charles asked.

"There's a strong possibility. Small-town life and all."

Just then, snow flurries fell from the sky like fairy dust.

"Would you look at that ..." he said.

Outside, the wind hastened upon stark tree limbs and howled to the full moon, now hidden from view. The young couple resumed their journey down the sidewalk as snow-flakes floated and danced all around them.

Charles fastened his grip on Rita. He tenderly traced her bare neck with soft fingers.

"Looks like they found that ol' Cape May magic," he whispered in her ear.

Mission accomplished, Rita thought.

Thank you for reading A CAPE MAY CHRISTMAS STORY. Receive a colorful **FREE recipe book** filled with some of the yummy treats, meals, and beverages mentioned throughout the story.

Go to www.suzannesimonetti.com and click on the Subscribe tab at the top of the screen.

*E-book readers: CLICK HERE to subscribe!

RECIPES

FROM

A Cape May Christmas Story

A CELEBRATION OF FAMILY AND LOVE IN AMERICA'S FIRST SEASIDE RESORT

by Suzanne Simonetti
USA Today bestselling author of *The Sound of Wings*

RITA'S HOT CHOCOLATE

This rich and warm wintry drink, widely celebrated in modern times, goes back to 500 BC. The Mayans drank chocolate made from ground-up cocoa seeds mixed with water, cornmeal, and chili peppers, making it a much different version from the hot chocolate we know today.

In the early 1500s, the explorer Cortez brought cocoa beans and chocolate drink-making tools to Europe where the beverage gained popularity and was adopted by the court of King Charles V, as well as by the Spanish upper class.

When it hit London in the 1700s, chocolate houses (similar to today's cafes) became popular and quite trendy, even though chocolate was very expensive. Up until the 19th century, hot chocolate was used as a treatment for stomach and liver diseases.

Today, we sip and savor the warm beverage as a favorite treat on cold nights by the fire, après-ski or ice skating, and throughout the Christmas season.

INGREDIENTS

- 4 cups milk (preferably whole or 2%)
- ¼ cup unsweetened cocoa powder
- 1 tablespoon granulated sugar (or your favorite sugar substitute)
- ½ cup bittersweet or semisweet chocolate chips or chopped chocolate bar
- ¼ teaspoon pure vanilla extract

DIRECTIONS

- Place milk, cocoa powder, and sugar in a small saucepan. Heat over medium/medium-low heat, whisking frequently, until warm (but not boiling). Add chocolate chips, and whisk constantly until they melt and distribute evenly into the milk. Whisk in vanilla extract, and serve immediately.

TIPS

- Add mini marshmallows for more of a treat.
- Top with whipped cream and crushed candy cane.
- Add a dollop of liquor if you wish: Kahlúa, peppermint schnapps, rum, or whiskey.

NONNA'S ITALIAN WEDDING SOUP

Minestra Maritata, meaning "wedded soup" in Italian. Research shows the dish may have originated in the Southern Italian region of Campania, linked to traditional rituals in various incarnations. Other research refers to it as an ancient Neapolitan soup.

Despite the moniker, the dish is not served at Italian weddings. It refers to its inexpensive meat and leafy greens that make up the main ingredients. The nuanced flavors are betrothed as they are blended and simmered, achieving a polygamy of meat, broth, and leafy greens.

For fun, I attributed it to Rita's Nonna in the story, since it's a personal favorite in our home.

INGREDIENTS

MEATBALLS

- 1 large egg
- ⅓ cup of fresh parsley
- 2 cloves garlic, minced
- 1 lb. 85 or 90% lean ground beef or turkey
- ½ cup grated Parmigiano Reggiano
- ⅓ cup Italian-seasoned breadcrumbs
- ½ teaspoon onion powder
- ¼ teaspoon salt
- ¼ teaspoon pepper

Soup

- 2 tablespoons olive oil
- 1 medium yellow onion, diced
- 2 large carrots, diced
- 2 stalks celery, diced
- 6 cups high-quality chicken broth
- 2 cups high-quality beef broth
- 2 cups water
- ½ cup dry white wine (optional)
- 1 bay leaf
- ½ teaspoon salt
- ¼ teaspoon white pepper (okay to use black pepper)
- 1 cup small pasta
- 6 oz. fresh escarole (or fresh spinach)
- Parmigiano Reggiano, for serving

INSTRUCTIONS

- Preheat the oven to 350°F.
- Line a baking sheet with aluminum foil and set an oven-proof roasting rack over top. Spray the rack generously with nonstick cooking spray.
- In a large bowl, beat the egg with the parsley and garlic. Add the remaining meatball ingredients and mash with your hands until evenly combined.
- Roll the mixture into tablespoon-sized balls, about 1 inch in diameter (it will make approximately 50 meatballs), and place on the prepared rack.
- Bake for 15 to 18 minutes, or until lightly browned and cooked through. Set aside.

- In a large soup pot or Dutch oven over medium heat, heat the olive oil.
- Add the onions, carrots, and celery and cook, stirring frequently, until the vegetables are softened, about 8 minutes.
- Add the chicken broth, beef broth, water, wine, bay leaf, salt, and pepper and bring to a boil.
- Add the pasta and cook, uncovered, at a gentle boil until the pasta is al dente, 8 to 10 minutes (or according to package directions).
- Taste the soup and adjust the seasoning, if necessary.
- Reduce the heat to low, and add the spinach and meatballs.
- Simmer for a few minutes, until the spinach is wilted and the meatballs are warmed through.
- Ladle into bowls, and serve with grated Parmigiano Reggiano.

TIPS
- You can substitute fresh spinach for the escarole, which isn't always available.
- Freezer-friendly instructions: The soup can be frozen for up to 3 months, but wait until you reheat the soup to add the pasta. Defrost the soup in the refrigerator for 12 hours, and then reheat it on the stovetop over medium heat until simmering, add the pasta, and cook until the pasta is tender.

CHRISTINA'S COQUITO – "PUERTO RICAN EGGNOG"

Coquito, meaning "little coconut" in Spanish, is a traditional Christmas drink that began in Puerto Rico. The coconut-based alcoholic beverage is a variation of traditional eggnog, whose roots go back to medieval Britain, known as posset.

INGREDIENTS

SPICED TEA (CLOVE WATER)
- 1 cup coconut water or filtered water
- 3 cinnamon sticks
- 2 star anise
- 1 vanilla bean split
- 1 teaspoon whole cloves
- ½ teaspoon allspice berries

COQUITO
- 1 can cream of coconut (15 oz.)
- 1 can sweetened condensed milk (14 oz.)
- 1 can coconut milk (13.5 oz.)
- 1 can evaporated milk (12 oz.) OR 1 can coconut milk (for additional coconut flavor)
- 1 teaspoon pure vanilla extract
- 3 cups rum (preferably white, but can use gold and/ or spiced rum, if desired.)
- 1 ½ teaspoons ground cinnamon

- ¼ teaspoon ground nutmeg
- 4 large, fresh egg yolks (This is optional. I've read that eggs are not used in classic Puerto Rican coquito, but some people enjoy the added thickness, which lends itself to the feel and taste of more traditional eggnog.)
- pinch kosher salt (optional)
- glass bottles for storing and gifts (optional)

DIRECTIONS FOR SPICED TEA (CLOVE WATER)

Can be made 1 week ahead.

- In a small saucepan combine the coconut water, cinnamon sticks, star anise, vanilla bean, cloves, and allspice berries.
- Bring the water to a boil over medium-high heat. Boil the tea for 1-2 minutes. Turn the stove off and allow the tea to steep for 15 minutes.
- Strain the spices from the tea, and press the paste from the vanilla into the strained tea.
- Set aside to flavor.

DIRECTIONS FOR COQUITO

- Add the spiced tea, ground cinnamon, nutmeg, and salt to blender.
- Add the cream of coconut, condensed milk, coconut milk, evaporated milk, vanilla extract, and rum to the blender.
- Optional: If you're adding egg yolk, do so now.
- Blend this mixture for 1 minute on low speed.

- Use a rubber spatula to scrape the sides of the blender, then blend for an additional 30 seconds to 1 minute on medium speed.
- Strain the coquito through a cheesecloth-lined funnel into a large pitcher to remove excess foam from the liquid. Discard the cheesecloth.
- Pour the strained coquito into the bottles, leaving at least 1 inch of headspace in each bottle.
- Cap the bottles and refrigerate for at least 48 hours to age.
- 10 to 15 minutes prior to serving, remove the bottle of coquito from the refrigerator to allow the fat in the coquito to warm up.
- Give the mixture a vigorous shake to blend the spices that will have settled. Serve cold with a sprinkle or grating of cinnamon and a cinnamon stick.

TIPS
- The alcohol will cure the coquito for at least a year, maybe longer.
- You can reduce the amounts of rum to one-half for less alcohol or eliminate altogether by adding more coconut milk.
- If the mixture is still very thick after allowing it to warm, try blending it again.

GRANDMA ABERNATHY'S
SCOTTISH MINCED PIE

During the Victorian Era, minced pie became a typical recipe for the Christmas holiday. Today, it is one of the most popular desserts in the United Kingdom, especially during the month of December. *Fun fact: Oliver Cromwell banned festive celebrations including minced pies and puddings during his short reign in the 1650s. Fortunately, the rule didn't last past his reign, and minced pies remain a Christmas tradition in the UK.

INGREDIENTS
- 1 ½ pounds lean ground beef
- 1 large onion, minced
- ⅛ teaspoon beef bouillon granules
- 4 cups water to cover
- 2 tablespoons cornstarch
- ¼ cup water
- Pastry dough for a 9-inch double crust pie

DIRECTIONS
- Place the ground beef in a large pot, and pour in enough water to cover beef. Boil until beef is cooked through. Drain.
- Add water to cover cooked beef, add onions and enough bouillon granules to taste.

- Cook until the onions are soft.
- Season with salt and pepper to your taste, and make sure the filling has enough bouillon for a nice beef flavor.
- Combine the ¼ cup water with the cornstarch, and stir until smooth.
- Add to the beef mixture, and cook until mixture has thickened.
- Allow to cool to room temperature.
- Preheat oven to 375°F (190°C).
- Roll out pastry to fit a 9-inch pie plate.
- Pour beef mixture into the pastry crust, and cover the top with pastry dough. Crimp edges and prick top.
- Bake in preheated oven until pie crust is lightly browned, about 40 minutes.

CHASE'S SPICED MULLED WINE

The first traces of mulled wine date back to medieval times. It is said the Romans and Greeks heated wine with spices to shield their bodies from chilly weather. The traditional preparation involves whole spices like cinnamon, which is known to have medicinal benefits.

The love for mulled wine grew enormously throughout the Middle Ages. Europeans gave it a unique twist by adding herbs and flowers for that extra sweetness. Many countries came up with their own variations to the traditional drink.

Just like decorated trees and Advent wreaths, mulled wine became a deeply rooted Christmas tradition in Germany that is now enjoyed around the world. A steaming hot mug of mulled wine is synonymous with wintry and seasonal festivities.

INGREDIENTS
- Wine
- Brandy (Rum, vodka, or leave it out altogether.)
- Oranges (or clementines or lemons or both.)
- Spices (Whole cloves or star anise and whole cinnamon sticks. Add whatever you have on hand, but take care to remove all spices before serving.)
- ¼ cup of honey

STOVETOP METHOD

- Combine all ingredients in a pot or saucepan set over medium heat.
- Gently bring the wine to a low simmer over medium-low heat. Do not boil. Heat for approximately 15-20 minutes, stirring occasionally.
- To serve, carefully ladle into the desired number of serving glasses. Leave the spices behind for re-use.
- Garnish with additional fruit, if desired.

SLOW COOKER/CROCKPOT METHOD

- Add all of the ingredients to a 4-quart slow cooker.
- Cover and heat on LOW for 1 hour, or until the wine is warm throughout.
- Ladle into glasses, leaving behind any spices.
- Garnish with fruit, if desired.

TIPS

- Can use red or white but this is traditionally made with an inexpensive red wine.
- Avoid over-spicing. Cinnamon sticks and whole star anise are potent. A couple of each is all you'll need.
- Avoid boiling. Boil for longer than a few seconds and you'll quickly decrease the overall alcohol content of your spiced wine.

GRAMMI'S GINGERBREAD
COOKIES FOR SANTA

GINGERBREAD IS A BAKED SWEET CONTAINING GINGER and sometimes cinnamon, cloves, nutmeg, cardamom, and anise. It can be sweetened with any combination of brown sugar, molasses, light or dark corn syrup, or honey. In the 16th century, the English replaced breadcrumbs with flour and added eggs and sweeteners, resulting in a lighter product. The first gingerbread man is credited to Queen Elizabeth I, who knocked the socks off visiting dignitaries by presenting them with one baked in their own likeness.

What is the difference between gingersnaps and gingerbread? Both are spiced cookies. Gingersnaps are typically rolled into balls, while gingerbread is rolled out and cut into shapes. Gingersnaps are also baked slightly longer, which is where they get their snappy crispiness. Gingerbread is typically a little chewier.

INGREDIENTS
- 1 cup plus 2 tablespoons unsalted butter, softened
- 1 cup packed brown sugar
- 1 egg
- ¼ cup plus 2 tablespoons molasses
- 2 ½ cups all-purpose flour
- 2 ¼ teaspoons baking soda

- ½ teaspoon kosher (coarse) salt
- 1 tablespoon ground ginger
- 1 tablespoon ground cinnamon
- 2 teaspoons ground cloves
- 1 ½ teaspoons ground nutmeg
- ½ teaspoon ground allspice
- ⅔ cup granulated or coarse sugar

DIRECTIONS

- Pre-heat oven to 350°F
- In large bowl, beat butter and brown sugar with electric mixer on medium speed until light and fluffy, about 5 minutes.
- Beat in egg and molasses.
- Stir in remaining ingredients except granulated sugar.
- Cover; refrigerate at least 2 hours.
- Line cookie sheets with cooking parchment paper or silicone baking mat.
- In small bowl, place granulated sugar.
- Shape dough into 1-inch balls; roll in sugar.
- On cookie sheets, place balls 2 inches apart.
- Bake 8 to 10 minutes or just until set and soft in center.
- Cool 2 minutes; from cookie sheets to cooling racks.
- Let cool on baking sheets for 5 minutes before transferring to a cooling rack to cool completely.

SUZANNE'S EGGPLANT LASAGNA

This one can be messy but is fairly inexpensive and filling, making it a great addition to your menu for small or large gatherings. We've come to love it all year round as a lighter variation of traditional lasagna.

INGREDIENTS
- 3 medium-sized ripe eggplants
- 5-6 small eggs or 3 large ones
- Italian-seasoned breadcrumbs
- Whole ricotta cheese (15 oz.)
- Tomato sauce (32 oz. of your favorite brand or homemade sauce)
- Shredded mozzarella cheese
- 4 cups olive oil

DIRECTIONS
- Pre-heat oven to 325°F (163°C).
- Cut eggplant into ¼ inch pieces.
- Whisk eggs.
- Add 2 cups of olive oil into pan over medium heat.
- Dip eggplant into egg and coat with breadcrumbs.
- Cook for 3-5 minutes on each side or until slightly browned and crisp.
- Drain eggplant on paper towels in layers.

- Take a few ounces of sauce and coat the bottom of a 9 x 13-inch baking dish.
- Place a layer of eggplant along the bottom.
- Spread ricotta onto eggplant.
- Cover with tomato sauce.
- Sprinkle mozzarella cheese.
- Add another layer of eggplant and repeat the process, finishing with the mozzarella cheese.

TIPS
- It is perfectly fine if you wish to salt your eggplant first. Some do that to cut back on bitterness and remove excess water.
- You may peel the skins, if you wish.

I hope you enjoy looking through the recipes. Wishing all my followers, readers, and friends a joyful and DELICIOUS holiday season.

Merry Christmas and Happy Holidays,
Suzanne Simonetti

HOT SPOTS

Please enjoy this list of the many restaurants, businesses, shops, churches, and points of interest. Many are mentioned throughout the story. (*Be sure to check hours of operation as some businesses are closed in the off-season but are captured in the story (e.g., *Hot Dog Tommy's*).

410 Bank Street	www.410bankstreet.com
Atlantic Cape Community College	https://www.atlanticcape.edu/
Barrier Island Books & Art	West Perry Street West Cape May
Borough Hall of West Cape May	www.westcapemay.us
Calvary Chapel Cape May	https://www.cccapemay.org/
Cape Atlantic Book Company	www.capeatlanticbookco.com
Cape Island Baptist Church	http://www.cibcnj.org/
Cape May Carriage Company	https://www.capemaycarriage.com/
Cape May Chamber of Commerce	www.capemaychamber.com
Cape May County Library	https://cmclibrary.org/
Cape May Food Closet	https://www.cmfoodcloset.org/
Cape May Lutheran Church	https://www.capemaylutheran.org/

Cape May Magazine	www.capemaymag.com
Cape May Olive Oil Company	capemayoliveoilcompany.com
Cape May Point Science Center	https://www.capemaypointscience-center.org/
Cape May Post Office	700 Washington Street Cape May
Cape May Presbyterian Church	https://www.capemaypresbyterian.com/
Cape May Stage	https://capemaystage.org/
Cape May United Methodist Church	https://capemayumc.org/
Cape May Vacation Properties (The Lorelei and John T. Craig House)	www.capemayvacationproperties.com
Cape May-Lewes Ferry	www.cmlf.com
Cape Mayniac	www.cape-mayniac.square.site
Carney's	www.carneysnj.com
Coffee Tyme	www.coffeetymenj.com
Congress Hall	www.caperesorts.com/congress-hall.com
Convention Hall	www.capemay.com/play/cape-may-convention-hall
Delaney's Irish Pub & Grill	www.delaneyscapemay.com
East Lynne Theater Company	https://www.eastlynnetheater.org/
Emlen Physick Estate	https://capemaymac.org/experience/emlen-physick-estate/
Episcopal Church of the Advent	https://capemayadvent.org/
Exit Zero Filling Station	www.exitzero.com
Grana BYOB	www.granabyob.com
Harry's Ocean Bar & Grille	www.harryscapemay.com
Hot Dog Tommy's	www.hotdogtommys.com
Iccara Italian Bistro	www.iccaracapemay.com

Janet Payne Jewelry	www.janetpaynejewelry.com
La Mer Beachfront Hotel/Pier House Restaurant	capemaylamer.com
Love the Cook	https://www.lovethecook.com/
Lucky Bones Back Water Grille	www.luckybones.com
Macedonia Baptist Church	630 Lafayette Street
Madame's Port	www.madamesport.com
Maison Bleue Bistro	www.maisonbleuebistro.com
Mid Atlantic Center for the Arts & Humanities (MAC)	www.capemaymac.org
Morey's Piers & Water Parks	http://www.moreyspiers.com/
Ostara's Coffe House	www.ostarascoffeehouse.business.site
Our Lady Star of The Sea Catholic Church	https://www.starofthesea.net/
Oyster Bay Restaurant Bar & Grille	www.oysterbayrestaurant.com
Peanut Butter Co.	www.capemaypeanutbutterco.com
Peter Shields Inn	www.petershieldsinn.com
Primal BYOB	www.primalcapemay.com
Southern Mansion	www.southernmansion.com
Spirit Catcher Photography	www.facebook.com/spiritcatcher-photography
Splash	www.whalestalecapemay.com
Taco Cabolito	https://www.tacocaballitotequileria.com/
The Branches Outreach Center of Rio Grande	https://www.thebranchesoutreach.org/
The Cricket Club	www.capemaycricketclub.com
The Emlen Physick Estate	www.capemaymac.org/experience/emlen-physick-estate
The Lobster House	www.thelobsterhouse.com

The Lookout at Ferry Park	www.visitferrypark.com
The Mad Batter Bar & Restaurant	www.madbatter.com
The Magic Brain Cafe	www.magicbraincapemay.com
The Nature Center of Cape May	www.njaudubon.org/centers/nature-center-of-cape-may
The Rusty Nail	www.caperesorts.com/capemay/rusty-nail
The Santa Express (Tuckahoe Village)	www.the-santa-express.com
The Squares	www.facebook.com/SquaresCape-May
West Cape May Christmas Parade	www.capemay.com/calendar/events/the-west-cape-may-christmas-parade
West End Garage	www.caperesorts.com/capemay/west-end-garage
Whale's Tale	www.whalestalecapemay.com
Wildwood Catholic Academy	https://www.wildwoodcatholicacademy.org/

ACKNOWLEDGMENTS

So much goes into the creation of a book, well beyond the simple craft of writing. This book is dedicated to my readers, and there are many who deserve honorable mention.

To my neighbor and friend, Kathy Brown, and the *Wines and Spines Book Club*. The day we met at *Lucky Bones* would have been my late father's eightieth birthday. Your smiling faces and warm hearts reminded me of the bounty that follows me throughout this lifetime. I cherish and thank you all with my whole heart.

Gratitude for my neighbors to the south, namely Sandy Bancroft and *The Devonswood Ladies Book Club* of North Carolina. This spirited bunch took a vote when we were deciding on a title for this story. Congratulations to our winner and organizer, Leslie Kirkwood, (and to my husband, Joe) for coming up with the title!. A special thank you to my friend, Linda Metcalf, and the *River Oaks Raleigh Book Club*.

There is no gentle way to express my gratitude for the gale-force winds at my back within the writing community. Thank you to my beloved gal pals and West Coast authors,

Patti Davis and Leslie Rasmussen—these two talented Libras keep me grounded and laughing all the while.

Thank you to friends and street team members who have guided me along this journey with know-how, advice, and contacts, including Liani Kotcher (writing as Rektok Ross), Meg Nocero, Valerie Taylor, Annette Glahn (writing as Annette G. Anders), Libby Jordan, Eryk Hanut, Diana Kupershmit, and beta reader Tammy Pasterick.

Many thanks and appreciation to my team of editors and designers: Amy Tipton of *Feral Girl Books*, Danna Steele of *Dearly Creative*, Stephanie Elliot, and Kelsey Spence.

There are special people in Cape May who continue to support me along the way. Big hugs to all of my neighbors for their continued support and enthusiasm. Sending love to my dear friend, Mary Ann Castagnetta of the *Cape Atlantic Book Company*, who makes a cameo in this story. (My depiction of her is accurate. Mary Ann gives the best hugs and book recommendations.) Janet Payne of *Janet Payne Jewelry* and Tina Giaimo of *Spirit Catcher Photography* fill me with their inspiration through their inimitable crafts, jewelry, and photography. Thank you to Kathleen Hayes and Kate Conley Chadwick of *Cape May Magazine*, and to my friend, Lori Sukenik Lazan, owner of the newly refurbished *John F. Craig House* on Columbia Avenue and winner of the 2022 Historic House Tour Award for *The Lorelei* on Perry Street. A shout-out to fellow authors and friends, Miles Nelson and Laura Quinn, who have riveting and beautiful stories set in Cape May. High-fives and gratitude to Johnny

Glogowski for a super fun and productive early morning shoot on Poverty Beach and Convention Hall.

My siblings, Elizabeth and Scott, are testimony to the goodness that is woven through the fabric of my life. No matter the darkness that befalls our family, the three of us remain a formidable alliance as we discover, evolve, and climb to the summit of our dreams. I am grateful for my two loudest and proudest cheerleaders.

Love and appreciation for my two favorite Christmas babies: my mother, Maggie, born on December 27, which falls on the night of the Full Cold Moon, and my mother-in-law, Adeline, born on December 2, the day of the *West Cape May Christmas Parade*. An extra-special squeeze to our newest family member, Claire Ruby. One day, you'll be old enough to read Glammi's stories, and she'll show you how to uncover the magic of all your big-girl wishes and dreams.

Being married to an author comes with a unique set of sacrifices, and Joe never complains. You are my real-life hero for countless reasons—including, but not limited to the small piles of clean laundry waiting for me every day and a half, and the endless loads of dishes you tackle. No one gets me as well as you do. Thank you for being the best sport imaginable and traversing mountains alongside me on this wild ride. Together we are everything. I love you.

ABOUT THE AUTHOR

 Suzanne Simonetti is the USA Today best-selling author of *The Sound of Wings* which is also set in Cape May. She lives on Cape May Harbor with her husband. For updates on her latest releases and giveaways, visit suzannesimonetti.com.